Karen lifted her chin, trying to keep her emotions from getting in the way of good sense.

"I need to be honest, Eric. After talking last night, I really think that—"

"I'm sorry about last night. I know I sounded like an unemployed womanizer, but that's not true. Please trust me. When you get to know me better, you'll see who I am. Don't think I'm a bad guy because my grandfather's a little gruff."

She bit back her desire to question his "a little gruff" comment then had second thoughts. The look on Eric's face and the sincerity in his eyes made her remember God's Word. "Do not judge, or you too will be judged." She hadn't given Eric or his grandfather a chance. "Why should I trust you?"

GAIL GAYMER MARTIN lives with her real-life hero and husband, Bob, in Lathrup Village, Michigan. Once a high school English and public speaking teacher, later a guidance counselor, Gail retired and taught English and speech at Davenport University. Now she is a full-time, award-winning writer of inspirational romance and women's fiction and the author of nineteen church resource books. Her first romance novel was published by Barbour in 1998, and in three years God has blessed her with nearly thirty novel and novella sales.

Books by Gail Gaymer Martin

HEARTSONG PRESENTS

HP302—Seasons
HP330—Dreaming of Castles
HP462—Secrets Within
HP489—Over Her Head

Out on a Limb

Gail Gaymer Martin

Heartsong Presents

To Marianne whose family's farm in Flushing, Michigan, became the inspiration for the setting of this story, and to the real Nadine Smith and all Heartsong readers who make writing Christian romance a true blessing.

A note from the Author:
I love to hear from my readers! You may correspond with me by writing:

> **Gail Gaymer Martin**
> **Author Relations**
> **PO Box 719**
> **Uhrichsville, OH 44683**

ISBN 1-59310-117-1

OUT ON A LIMB

Our mission is to publish and distribute inspirational products offering exceptional value and biblical encouragement to the masses.

one

The sun spilled a dappled pattern along the wood's leaf-strewn path. Balanced high up on an oak branch, Karen Chapman drew in a deep calming breath. Trees and meadows burdened with Michigan wildflowers soothed her city nerves. In another month she would return to the city and her difficult job of working with the courts as a child advocate. Still, no matter what tense moments lay ahead, today was heaven.

Though not yet September, autumn hung in the air. Karen leaned her back against the rough bark and breathed in the scent of ripe apples that drifted on the breeze from her grandfather's orchard. Overhead the green leafy canopy splattered with gold and red hinted of cooler days.

God's handiwork glowed in the afternoon sun, and a song lifted in her heart. "For the beauty of the earth, for the glory of the skies." She began to hum, thinking about her newly widowed grandpa back at the house and praising God that He'd guided her to come to the farm for a visit.

The words of another hymn spilled from her thoughts to her lips. "Earth and all stars," she sang then chuckled when she lilted the verse about "engines and steel" and "loud building workers." *Too much reality there,* she thought, recalling the Detroit suburb's constant construction and traffic noise. Her song echoed through the trees, arousing the birds and exhilarating her spirit.

"Very nice, lady in the tree."

The voice from below unsettled her. Karen jammed her lips together, cutting off the last syllable and gazed down at the man standing beneath her. "Sorry. I thought I was alone."

5

"No need to apologize. I heard you singing out here yesterday."

Heat rose to her cheeks, and she eyed the branches below her, wondering how to make a quick escape rather than face the embarrassing situation. She bit her lip, seeing no human way to vanish from the limb. "I guess I'd better keep my singing for church."

He rested his weight on one booted foot and leaned his fist against his trim, jeans-covered hip. A smile curved his full lips, and his chuckle rose to meet her. "Why? I like free concerts." He leaned against the tree. "Mind if I stick around and listen?"

"You can do what you like, I suppose, but the concert's over. Anyway, these aren't my woods." The woods belonged to her grandfather, however, and she almost told him so.

"I know."

She eyed him. "What do you mean?"

"I mean it's not your woods."

An uneasy feeling shuffled through her. She peered at him through the tree limbs. "It's not your woods either, I don't imagine." She cringed, calculating that she'd passed her grandpa's property line and was now sitting in the Kendalls' tree.

"This is my grandfather's land." He lifted an eyebrow, his broad hands on his hips.

She winced.

"Lionel Kendall. Do you know him?" he asked.

"Not really." But she remembered him, all right. He scared her when she was young. His grandfather and hers had been battling for years. Knowing who the stranger was, she wanted nothing to do with him or his grandfather. "Well, if that's the case, let me get out of your tree."

With what decorum Karen could muster, she edged her straddled leg over the limb and slid the other one down to the next branch. *So far so good.* Somehow, it seemed easier climbing up than down. When she attempted to guide her leg down to the next branch, she couldn't release her other foot. Her shoe had lodged in a deep, angular crook of the tree limb.

Her hot cheeks heated to boiling. As Karen struggled to move her bound leg, he stood below her, a teasing smirk twinkling on his face. His laughter traveled up the trunk faster than she was climbing down.

"Stuck?" he asked.

His voice reeked with humor. So much so, she refused to answer. What did he think? She wasn't hanging in the tree for fun.

He stepped forward and grasped a lower branch. "I guess you are. Let me help." He clutched a limb, raised himself, and swung his lean, nimble leg over the branch.

She wanted to refuse his assistance, but it was one of those "cut off your nose to spite your face" situations. She grasped the limb with one hand and, with the other, reached above and tugged wildly at her jammed shoe.

The branch she clutched dipped then lurched, and she clung like gum to a sole, praying she wouldn't fall to the ground. But falling would at least free her from the situation. The image made her smile.

The man loomed beside her, the muscles of his arms swelling as he raised himself to the branch above.

"Okay," he said, "let's slip your foot out of your shoe. Then I'll get it loose."

His large hand gripped her ankle while the other unlaced her sneaker. Finally, her foot escaped its prison. Wearing one shoe, she clambered down the branches to the ground, feeling like a child rescued by a cocky policeman.

At the same time, her liberator dropped to the ground beside her, his grin like the Cheshire cat. He lifted his arm and held out her scuffed sneaker. "Cinderella? I believe I have your glass slipper."

She snatched the shoe from his hand, too embarrassed to look him in the eye, and muttered, "Thank you." Spinning on her shoed foot, she hobbled down the sun-speckled path toward the orchard, her shoe clasped in her hand.

"You're very welcome," he called out after her. "And you don't have to run away, Cinderella. It's not anywhere near midnight."

His footsteps padded behind her, and the closer he got, the quicker she walked. Suddenly her stockinged foot landed on a jagged stone, and she released a loud "Ouch." But without a break in her step, she hobbled away.

"If you slowed down. . .or put on your shoe, you might save a doctor bill."

She'd reached the orchard and glanced over her shoulder. Now he was on *her* grandfather's property. A bough heavy with apples stood within arm's reach, and she snatched one off the limb and, with a glance, tossed it over her shoulder toward him.

"An apple a day keeps the doctor away," she called. For good measure, she plucked one for herself and, with a snap, sank her teeth into the sweet tangy pulp. She didn't stop until she reached the meadow, and when she did, he was gone. Like finishing a lovely novel, she felt disappointed it had ended.

❧

Eric Kendall stood between two apple trees and watched her stumble through the meadow like the nursery rhyme: "One shoe off and one shoe on. Diddle-Diddle Dumpling. . ." Except she wasn't his son John. He didn't know who she was, exactly, but he knew she was from the Chapman house.

What he did know was she had spunk. And a lovely face like sunshine with freckles. He'd been enchanted hearing her sing one of his favorite hymns the day before when he took a walk through the woods to stretch his legs when he first arrived. But she'd vanished before he found her.

He chuckled, thinking of her comical descent from the tree. She sure had her dander in an uproar. From the woman's attitude, he'd guess she was related to Walter Chapman. For years, his grandfather and Walter Chapman had some kind of ongoing feud, but he could never fathom the reason.

He snatched a stem of timothy and put it between his teeth and gazed ahead at his grandparents' familiar old farmhouse. Coming here was like a step back in time. He'd spent wonderful summers at the farm as a child, and right now he needed something to cling to. Something warm and soothing like his gramma's peanut butter cookies.

In the past three months, he'd ended a dead-end relationship and faced a new career right here in Gaylord, but one with financial risk. Change seemed to come in twos and threes. Never one change alone that he could handle. The failed relationship, he could deal with. It had been coming for a long time, and he felt confident the Lord had guided his direction.

Admitting his weakness, he had to confess that sometimes a gorgeous figure and beguiling smile got in the way of common sense. But before it was too late, he realized Janine's values were far from his own Christian beliefs. Like Grandmother always said, "Eric, listen to God's Word. Don't get yourself yoked up with an unbeliever." Those words had banged around in his head until he finally listened.

Nearing the house, he saw his grandmother bent over in the small garden filled with straight rows of green peppers, tomatoes, and cucumbers. His grandfather wouldn't be outdone with his neighbor's gardening attempts.

When his grandmother spotted him, she pushed a wisp of white hair from her cheek and grinned. "Where've you been?"

"Listening to a concert in the woods."

She nodded. "You mean the birds. They do sing a lovely tune."

Eric chuckled and bent down to pluck a handful of green beans and dropped them in her plastic bucket. "Not birds, Gramma. But she could've been, perched in the tree like that." He pictured the woman nestled on the branch, mottled with sun and shade, her voice floating to heaven.

His grandmother lifted her freed hand and rested her palm on his forehead. "Too much sun, Eric. You're having a heatstroke."

He laughed and yanked her apron string. The ties loosened, and the calico print slipped down her skirt.

She grabbed the apron before it hit the ground. "I should take you over my lap." Grinning, she swung the bucket toward him. "What are you talking about, anyway? Who was perched in a tree?"

"That's what I was going to ask you," Eric said, retrieving the apron from her hand. He wrapped it around her ample waist and retied the strings.

"How should I know?" she asked. "Did you see me hidin' in the bushes?"

"She must be a relative of Mr. Chapman. When she left, she headed back through the orchard with one shoe on and one shoe off." He chuckled.

"Now I know you've had too much sun," she said, wrapping her arm around his, as they headed back to the house. "I made up some lemonade. A cold drink might help those delusions you're havin'."

"Dark blond like ripe wheat. Freckles on her nose. And spunky like you, Gramma. Even meaner, maybe."

She squeezed his arm with a little shake. "You better watch out how you talk to me, young man. I can still wash your mouth out with soap."

"And she's almost as pretty as you, too."

"Go on," she said. "You're talkin' blarney now. You must've got those sweet talkin' Irish ways from my father." She patted his arm. " 'Cuz you sure didn't get them from your grandpa."

He pulled open the back door, and Bea walked into the kitchen. Eric followed and slid into the chair. "So who is she?"

Bea turned to face him. "You don't remember her? I'm

guessin' she's Karen. Walter said she was comin' for a visit. . .one day when he was sociable." She shook her head, followed by a patient grin. "I'm glad, too. He's not doin' well since his wife died nearly a year ago. Loneliness. Gets to everyone eventually."

Eric eyed her, wondering if she was talking about herself. "And Karen is. . . ?"

"His granddaughter. Remember the cute little thing who would come over with her grandmother sometimes when you came to visit? She'd sing a song at the drop of a hat. She always steered clear of your grandfather."

"Karen?" He sent his mind marching back in time. A faint vision drifted across his memory. He remembered once chasing a saucy little blond girl through the cornrows and when he caught her, he kissed her. His first kiss. He was six or seven, maybe. A grin slid onto his face.

Bea glanced at him over her shoulder then turned back to the sink, snapping and washing the beans. "What's that smile for?"

"Just thinking, Gramma. Granddad didn't plant corn this year, did he?"

"Corn? No, why?"

"No reason."

He remembered her clearly now. *Karen.* She was as cute and spunky twenty-some years ago as she was today, and picturing her darting through the meadow a short time ago, he knew she'd definitely outrun him in the cornrows now.

two

An apple a day keeps the doctor away. Karen wished she'd listened to her own advice and eaten the apple earlier. She sat in her bedroom, rubbing the bottom of her foot where she'd stepped on the rock. The foot had been bruised, she guessed.

She took a couple of practice steps, trying not to limp. Her grandfather would question her, and she didn't want to talk about her meeting with the Kendall man. Even mentioning the last name would rile her grandpa. She knew it.

Concentrating on not wincing, Karen headed into the kitchen to fix lunch, but before she got one foot through the doorway, her grandfather stood at the other end of the hall watching her.

"What's wrong with your foot?"

"Stepped on a stone," she said, continuing her journey through the doorway. She headed for the refrigerator and swung it open. She sensed her grandfather had followed behind her.

"Where were your shoes?"

She turned to face him, knowing an attempt to keep anything from the sharp eyes of her grandfather was pointless. "One was on my foot."

He ambled into the room and grasped the chair back, looking puzzled. "And the other?"

"In my hand."

A grin spread across his face, and he pulled out the chair and sat. "Sounds like an interesting story."

She pushed her head back into the refrigerator and mumbled a few words of explanation about a stranger upsetting ⁃ in the woods. When she pulled out a package of luncheon meats and the mayo jar, one bushy eyebrow had raised as he waited. Karen set the items on the table and returned for the lettuce. Then she faced him. "Wheat or sourdough?"

"Sourdough. . .with tomatoes, too."

Karen nodded and went back to the refrigerator for a tomato, hoping he'd forgotten the whole issue now that the conversation had changed to their lunch. She set about making the sandwiches without a word, feeling relieved as each second ticked away. She placed the sandwich in front of him on a paper plate. "Milk or lemonade?"

"Milk, and you have some, too," he said.

"I hate milk."

"It's good for you."

Karen gave up and poured him a tall glass and a few ounces for herself. She'd learned years ago that arguing with her grandfather seemed pointless. He could be stubborn as a tea stain on a white silk blouse.

She slid the glasses onto the table then sat. Her grandfather gave a blessing, and before she could echo his amen, he'd grabbed his sandwich.

A secret smile fought for recognition, but she kept it hidden, pleased she'd duped her grandfather into forgetting the conversation.

"Good sandwich," he said, wiping his mouth with a paper napkin he'd pulled from a holder.

"Thanks, Grandpa." Seeing him look content and less lonely made her day.

He laid the partially eaten sandwich back on the plate. "So tell me about the stranger in the woods."

She pulled her head upward, totally discouraged at his persistence. "Fine. Ruin your lunch."

"How's that?"

She knew what was coming. "He said his grandfather is Lionel Kendall. Now are you happy?"

His expression looked like he'd eaten a lemon coated with sawdust. His mouth puckered, then twisted as if he had words to say, but he couldn't spit them out.

"See, Grandpa. I ruined your lunch."

"Speaking of that old codger, he's stinkin' up my backyard. He's got to stop, or I'm callin' the police."

Karen set her sandwich down, her appetite already ruined. "Why is he stinking up your yard?"

"He puts his garbage along the fence close to my house. I can't even sit on the back porch."

The smell had never bothered Karen, but she knew her grandfather would make his own stink until they were removed. She hid her grin, amazed at his penchant for finding fault with Mr. Kendall. "I'll see what I can do, Grandpa. Now eat your lunch."

He dug into the last of his sandwich while she watched, wondering why she'd even tried to hide her stone bruise from him. If she'd told him when she'd first returned, the whole conversation would have been over, and they might have enjoyed their meal together. "Are you opening the vegetable stand this afternoon?"

"I might. I was out there for a couple of hours this morning. Not much traffic, but I figure the people passing from work might stop by this afternoon." He finished the last crust then swilled down the milk. "Thanks for lunch." He eyed her half-eaten meal, and his expression shifted. "Not hungry?"

She shrugged. "I don't like hearing you get so angry, Grandpa. If Grandma were here, she'd quote you Proverbs. 'A gentle answer turns away wrath, but a harsh word stirs up anger.' You'd dislike Mr. Kendall if he sat outside and read his Bible."

"The man doesn't own a Bible."

Karen shook her head as she rose and cleared the table. Her sandwich became garbage. She'd see what she could do about the trash barrels, but she didn't think the problem was as serious as her grandfather made it out to be. It was part of his unending quarrel with the neighbor.

❧

Eric drew a circle on the condensation covering his iced tea glass. His thoughts were going nowhere, just like the big O he'd etched on the tumbler. Sometimes his life seemed like a zero, but now he had plans to make a change, to make a difference.

When he lifted his eyes, he saw his grandmother's curious stare. He pulled away his gaze and saw the same look on his grandfather's face.

"What's troubling you?" Lionel asked.

Eric took a long drink of tea to give himself time to think. He had a wonderful plan, but he wasn't ready to tell his grandparents about it—not until he knew the deal was settled. He did have other news that had rocked his world until he felt God's hand on his heart and knew he had done the right thing.

"Nothing really. I'm just looking at some changes in my life."

"What kind of changes?" his grandmother asked, her plump face settling into a frown.

"Don't worry, Gramma. Some changes happened months ago."

"Then spit 'em out," his grandfather said, leaning a thick arm against the table. "Don't make us lollygag with wonderin'."

"I don't want you to be disappointed. That's all." He saw his granddad's pursed lips and decided to just tell them. "I broke up with Janine a few months ago."

"B—but I thought you were almost ready to give her a ring." The frown deepened on his grandmother's brow.

"I thought that was the way to go, but something about our relationship bothered me. Something kept niggling me until I put it in the Lord's hands. The answer came as clear as a spring morning."

Bea shifted her plate and rested her arms on the dining room table. "But what happened?" She paused a moment, then added, "If I'm not meddling."

Eric reached across the linen cloth and patted his gramma Bea's hand. "You're not meddling." He delved into the depth of his mind to answer the question. The reason had been more like a feeling than an actual revelation from God. He tried to recall all the deductions he'd made to come up with the decision. "We had different purposes in life, I think."

"She was a Christian."

Her sentence sounded like a question rather than a statement. "Yes. Janine went to church, but she looked at life with more of an earthly purpose than I did. I don't seem to care that much about money or owning fancy cars and houses. She does."

His gaze traveled across the room. The mahogany buffet lined with family photos, the worn carpet beneath the table, and the loving nicks hidden by the linen tablecloth—all these homey things meant more to him than most luxuries. "I love this farmhouse, Gramma, but Janine wouldn't want this. She'd want a modern house in the suburbs and a new car every year."

"Nothing wrong with new things," his grandfather muttered.

"You didn't need them, Granddad. You love the farm. . .and so do I."

His grandmother studied his face for a lengthy time then gave a decisive pat to the table. "Then you did the Lord's bidding. If you feel in your heart God guided your decision, you followed His will. That's all that matters."

"Thanks," Eric said, pleased to hear his grandmother's validation on his once uneasy decision.

His grandfather made a few grumbling sounds before he spoke. "Not sure a farm would do you any good nowadays. Most have gone fallow, but I trust your conviction, Eric. You've made your decision about Janine, and your grandmother and I hope you find another nice girl one day."

"Your grandfather and I were just talking about you being married and giving us some great-grandchildren." His grandmother gave him a gentle smile.

"I'm not opposed to marriage, Gramma. I just need to find the right girl."

"I know one—the best one," his grandfather said. He reached across the empty space and grasped Bea's arm with a shake. "You missed out on her, though." He gave a chuckle. "She's a little old for you, anyway."

Eric grinned at his grandfather's lighthearted banter and enjoyed it much more than his usual growl. He wished he could tell them his other news. In time he could. When the building deal came through, he'd delight in telling his grandparents he'd be moving to Gaylord—closer to them. Since his parents had moved to Arizona, Eric knew his grandparents were lonely for family.

His grandmother loosened herself from Lionel with a teasing slap. She rose and began scraping the dinner dishes. Eric followed her example and gathered a load, then carried them to the kitchen. As he helped with the scraps, Eric bundled the trash and tied the bag. "I'll take this outside."

"Thanks," she said as she rinsed the dishes beneath the tap.

Eric lifted the bag and stepped through the back door. The sun clung to the rooftops, spreading a fiery glow as it sank below the horizon. The air had cooled, and Eric drew in a deep breath, feeling whole and happy on the farm. He'd spent many summer days on the farm as a boy. So had Karen Chapman. The memories touched him again. They'd been summer playmates back then, despite the family feud raging strong.

The family feud. He wished he understood it.

He hoisted the white plastic bag and carried it across the lawn to the trash cans set along the fence. Eric eyed the containers, wondering why his grandfather put them so far from the house. Most people tucked them behind a shed or in a corner niche outside the house, but Granddad Lionel had lined them along the Chapman fence.

The answer struck him. Another "get even" for Granddad's silly bickering with Walter Chapman.

Eric lifted the lid and sank the bag into the metal can. As he lowered the lid, making sure it closed tightly, he heard a door slam and lifted his gaze. Karen strutted across the lawn like a warrior armed for battle. He considered grasping the trash can lid for a shield, but he noticed she had no visible weapon, no pitchfork or butcher knife, so he waited, unprotected from her wrath.

"Good evening," he said, watching her flared nostrils give a quick flutter.

"It might be good if you could do something with your grandfather."

He rested his hand on the white picket, admiring the flush of her cheeks. "What do you have in mind?"

Karen drew back then scowled. "I–you. . .how do I know? You should think of something. My grandfather is tired of these trash cans lining the fence. Why not put them around the corner of the house?" She swung her hand, indicating the location.

He glanced over his shoulder and saw the same place he'd been thinking about. "Good spot," he said and waited.

"Then?"

"They're not my trash barrels. I'll check with my granddad, but I'm sure this is the exact place he wants them. They wouldn't upset your grandfather if they were over there and out of the way."

Her proud shoulders slumped with resignation. "The feud. It's foolish."

"Look, I'll talk with him, but it's like talking to a mule. I doubt if he'll listen."

"I'd appreciate it."

"By the way, I'm Eric Kendall. I don't think we introduced ourselves." He grinned at her. "You're Karen. I. . .sort of remember you."

"Me, too." She stayed in place and looked at the grass. Her feet shifted from one side to the other, as if she had more to say. Finally she tilted her chin upward. "You really don't know what that whole feud thing is about?"

"Sorry. I don't have a clue. In fact, I'd wondered if you knew anything."

"Not a thing. Have you ever asked?"

He nodded. "Many times. Even my grandmother brushes it off and says they're just grumpy old men. I'm beginning to think it's like the legendary feuding families, the Hatfields and the McCoys. No one really remembers whether it was an argument over a pig or something else."

Karen's face broke into a smile. "I'm beginning to think the same thing."

He loved seeing her smile and wished she'd do it more often. "I'll see what I can do about the trash barrels, but don't count on it changing."

Kate stepped back and gave a nod. "I'd appreciate it."

Eric watched her saunter across the grass toward the back porch. Her stride was much slower and less determined as she walked away. He liked her looks.

Her looks? He liked Karen.

❧

Karen looked out the back porch window toward the Kendalls' fence. The trash cans were still sitting where they'd been yesterday. She shook her head. The battle wasn't worth the effort. She didn't smell a thing, and she guessed her grandfather didn't either. It was the principle.

Her grandfather's footsteps alerted her, and Karen headed back into the kitchen to greet him. "Coffee, Grandpa?"

He nodded and eyed the stove top.

"I made pancakes. They're keeping warm in the oven."

He gave a grin and settled at the table. In moments, she'd piled the golden-brown cakes on his plate and handed him a bottle of syrup she'd kept warm. He bowed his head and said a blessing over the food, then dug in.

"Are we setting up the produce stand this morning?" she asked.

He nodded then swallowed before speaking. "Friday's usually a good day, but I'm worried. The sky looks cloudy. They're rain clouds for sure."

"Gray skies can't hold us back, Grandpa. Are the vegetables in the shed?"

"Yep, and some pecks of apples."

"Let me get started while you finish up." Before he could direct her action, she hurried onto the porch and outside.

Grandpa was correct. The clouds had heavy gray bottoms and hid any blue that might be above them. An occasional shift by the wind let a fraction of sunlight through and gave Karen a sliver of hope. She loaded the hand truck with baskets of the produce her grandfather grew in his fields and headed down the driveway.

Minutes passed as she lifted the front cover of the stand to form a wooden awning, then unloaded the baskets with corn, tomatoes, carrots, peppers, and slender cucumbers just right for pickles. As she lifted a peck of apples to the counter, her grandfather arrived and set out the prices. Karen unfolded two canvas chairs, and they sat.

A car rolled passed, then stopped on the shoulder and backed up. Karen jumped up, and soon other vehicles parked to check out the produce. With purchases bagged, her grandfather harvested the money. When business slowed, they settled into the chairs again.

The conversation moved from the weather to her grandfather's health concerns, and lingered over stories about Karen's grandmother Hazel.

"Your grandma is everywhere in the house," her grandfather said.

Karen's stomach knotted. "I know, Grandpa. I picture Grandma in the kitchen, baking or canning. Sometimes both. The house always smelled of apples. Apple pies, apple jelly, apple kuchen. Even the memory makes my mouth water."

"She was a good cook, your grandma. . .and pretty as a lacy pillow."

Karen never thought of her grandmother as pretty. She recalled her as cuddly and loving. But when she thought back, Karen remembered seeing old photos of her grandma in her youth. She had been a pretty woman in her 1940s long straight dresses and wearing flowered hats and white gloves. Her grandmother had a lovely smile and eyes that glinted. Flirtatious eyes, they might be called today, but eyes with a pinch of mischief that welcomed everyone.

"She was pretty," Karen said, rethinking her earlier notion. "But she was so much more to me."

Her grandfather reached over and patted her hand. "She loved you so much. I remember her saying you'd make a beautiful bride one day." He tilted his head and gave her a questioning look. "No beaus in the picture, sweetheart?"

Karen felt a grin flicker on her mouth. "No. Not a one. You're the special man in my life now, Grandpa." She said the words, but her mind shifted to an image of Eric Kendall. Despite her efforts to push him out of her thoughts, they had a will of their own. Eric seemed to settle there daily, and she couldn't budge him. The feud didn't make her feel any easier.

The conversation soon quieted, but Karen's thoughts didn't. The silly business between her grandfather and Eric's still lingered in her mind. How could one argument last so long for a Christian man?

"Grandpa, I wish you'd explain your feud with Mr. Kendall. I keep protecting your rights, but I'd like to know what I'm defending. . .and why."

He brushed his hand across the air as if to erase her question.

"The man's ignorant and a rotten neighbor. Always was. Always will be."

As the words left his mouth, a raindrop struck Karen on the arm. She looked upward toward a black hovering cloud and rose as another larger drop struck her followed by another.

She leaped from the chair. "We'd better get this cleared away. Looks like that rain you were worried about decided to pay us a visit." As she spoke, Karen had already begun loading the vegetables into the baskets.

Her grandfather leaned on the counter and looked upward. "It's Lionel again. He's over there sticking pins in a carrot, just asking for rain. The man jinxed me again."

Karen looked heavenward. *Lord, help Grandpa understand that you are in charge of weather and of all things, not Mr. Kendall. And please, Father, if I can work a tiny miracle in Your name, let me be the catalyst that changes things here. I only have a few weeks, so make it fast, Lord.* Her amen hit her thought at the same time as a crack of lightning.

She jerked in surprise and wondered if the thunder was God saying "yes."

Or was the Lord threatening a "no"?

three

Karen wandered through the house, feeling trapped by the summer showers. She glanced out the window, watching the rain beat a steady stream against the lawn and roll in rivulets from the porch roof. *Stopped-up eaves troughs,* she thought. One day she'd check that out. She didn't want her grandfather climbing a ladder to clean the gutters.

Bored, she wandered into the kitchen and stared into the refrigerator. She'd bake something if she had the ingredients and a recipe. Cookies sounded good or maybe a cake. With pies, she was hopeless.

"I'm going to the grocery store," Karen called to her grandfather from the kitchen doorway. "Need anything?"

She heard him mumbling and finally a response. "Check the bread and milk. Oh, and peanut butter. I've been hungry for a peanut butter and jelly sandwich."

"Okay," she called. She grabbed her handbag and an umbrella. Even getting wet was better than getting nowhere. That's what she'd been doing since the rain started.

❧

Eric leaped from his SUV and ran into Glen's Market. He'd wanted an excuse to come into town and ended up with his grandmother's grocery list. His trip was motivated by curiosity. He hadn't heard from the Realtor and was anxious to learn if he'd had a counteroffer on the property. The man had no added news but promised to make a telephone call and get back to Eric.

Though he wanted nothing more than to tell his grandparents, even tell Karen, about his plans, he cautioned himself

23

in doing so. As soon as he opened his mouth, he was sure he'd get complaints and people's advice. He didn't want that now. Eric had thought long and hard. He'd done his homework; he'd looked for a bargain and a good location. He'd done everything to make this endeavor a success. Besides all that, he feared competition. A good idea could be stolen as easily as a bicycle left on the sidewalk.

When he reached the entrance, he stomped his wet feet on the mat inside the door, grabbed a cart, and hauled out his list. As he passed the produce, he couldn't help but think of his plan. He'd dreamed for the past few years of opening a natural food and health product market in town. He wanted to include homegrown produce, too. So many of the farmers had given up farming, but those who still did had no efficient outlet for their products except at the roadside stands. Rain, cold, and busy highways made their job difficult, but in Eric's market, he could offer customers a pleasant atmosphere to purchase homemade jams and canned pickles, as well as fresh in-season crops. Everyone loved homegrown food.

He paused a moment at the meat counter, then pushed away and headed down the next aisle. As he looked ahead, he noticed a familiar face at the far end. *Karen.* Even her name made his pulse skip a beat. He shook his head at his lack of control. She had no interest in a man who'd just broken up with a woman and was about to give his last shirt for a new business. Anyway, she hated him, he feared.

That fact settled uneasily in his chest. He liked Karen, and if he had a chance, he'd like to pursue getting to know her better. While his reasoning told him to back off, his heartbeat shifted to high gear, and he found himself moving past the food displays to catch up with her. He swung around the corner and headed two aisles over. He figured they'd meet in the middle of the aisle.

He was right. As soon as he took a few steps, Karen came

around the far corner. With her eyes focused on the food display, she didn't see him until they were cart nose to cart nose. When she looked up, her face filled with surprise.

"Hi," he said, unable to think of anything more original.

"What are you doing here?" she asked, a questioning look in her eye.

He suspected she thought he'd followed her. "I'm not having my tires rotated," he said. As soon as the words left his mouth he'd wished they hadn't.

Karen's frown deepened, and to cover his dumb comment, he waved his grandmother's grocery list in the air. "I'm picking up a few items for the family."

"Me, too," she said, not waving anything. She turned her eyes toward the shelving and grasped a large jar of chunky peanut butter.

Eric peered at his empty cart and did the same. He set down the jar and stared at his list for a moment to gather his thoughts. "We needed the rain," he said, wondering why he'd mentioned it.

"Grandpa thinks your grandfather put a jinx on the weather. We had to close down the stand today because of the storm."

Eric felt his eye's widen. "And he blamed my grandfather?"

"Naturally." She propped her hand against her hip and shook her head. "Nonsense, but that's what he does."

Thinking about his market concept, Eric couldn't resist the moment. "It's too bad when summer's so short and the small farmer has to deal with weather problems."

"It is," she said, shifting past him and stopping at the canned goods.

Eric checked his list and followed. He saw no canned goods on the list, but he grabbed a tin of pinto beans. His grandmother would use them somehow, and he had to appear as if he were actually shopping.

"People look forward to buying fresh produce. I always consider homegrown fruits and vegetables the best," he said, studying her face.

"Right, but it's a short season."

"Short, and then add the rainy days. Farmers have problems."

She nodded and rolled the basket ahead of him.

She paused. "Aren't you going the wrong way? I thought you just came from this direction."

The truth hit him between the eyes. "When I saw you, I stopped shopping." The words flew past his lips.

"I'll take that as a compliment."

"Good," he said, feeling tongue-tied.

"I thought maybe you were following me," she said.

"Me? Follow you?" A sound left his throat between a laugh and a choke. "I'm shopping just like you are." He dropped another couple of items into his basket.

She looked into his basket and chuckled. "Baby shampoo?"

He cringed. He'd grabbed without looking. Eric had no answer that made sense, so he peered at his list and shrugged. He followed along, making an occasional comment, and when she made another reference to the rain, he eased in his last question. "Wouldn't it be nice to have a store that specialized in homegrown products? A place where people could buy them and not have to worry about the weather?" He felt a smile grow, anxious for her response.

She only shrugged. "I've never given it any thought."

He felt his face contort from a smile to a frown. "No, but it's a good idea. Don't you think?"

"I don't think it would impress people. . .especially not the farmers."

He thought it would please the local farmers, but how could he explain without telling her his plan? Karen's comment twisted his stomach in knots. Nevertheless, he tucked her words into the back of his mind. Rather than rebut her comment, he changed the subject. "Sorry about the trash cans."

"I noticed they weren't moved."

"Granddad had a million reasons why that's exactly where they should be. I'll try to talk with him some other time. He was in a mood yesterday."

"Like always, from what I heard." She manipulated her basket to get past his.

Eric blocked her. "Granddad is more bark than bite. You don't really know him."

"And not sure I want to."

When the words left her mouth, Eric noticed a look of repentance on her face. He waited.

"Sorry. I'm reiterating what Grandpa says. I don't really know your grandfather at all since I've become an adult. When I was a child, he just scared me a little."

He smiled. "One day you should stop by. I know you like my grandmother. At least you did when we were kids."

Karen's face brightened. "I do. She was always kind and sweet to us. She slipped us treats. Remember?"

He recalled. Despite his parents' warning, Gramma did a lot to develop Eric's sweet tooth.

Karen eyed her cart. "I need to be on my way. Grandpa will wonder where I am."

Eric shifted his cart. "See you over the back fence. . .or out on a limb."

A knowing grin spread across her face.

Eric watched her go, admiring her fair hair that rolled under at the ends and her trim form that bounced when she walked. He liked Karen—too much for his own good. But he knew himself too well. No family feud or discouragement would stop him. When he felt the Lord's hand on his arm, Eric accepted that God was moving him forward, and Eric was eager to move.

Maybe more quickly than God had planned, but Eric couldn't stop himself.

Karen pulled the batch of cut-and-bake cookies out of the oven. They were less work than making her own from scratch, and she could still say she baked them. That part was the truth. She grinned at her silly thought. Who cared?

When she'd gotten home, Granddad had decided to take a nap, but the smell roused him. He passed her in the kitchen doorway as she headed for the living room with a napkin full of warm goodies. Before she sat, Karen paused in front of an old bookcase, studying the book titles. As she scanned the covers, she noticed a stack of photo albums and scrapbooks on the bottom shelf. She set the cookies on a lamp table and pulled out one of the photograph books.

After settling onto the sofa, she nibbled the sweets and flipped the pages. Old pictures of her grandmother and grandfather intrigued her. This album held pictures of when they were young, probably high school or even earlier. Occasionally they stood with a group of friends, and Karen let her mind travel, imagining what their lives might have been like all those years ago. Her grandmother had died too young. She'd been a vital young woman, according to the photographs. She gazed at pictures of them on horseback and tobogganing. Each one made her more curious.

"Good cookies," her grandfather said, coming through the doorway.

"Thanks. I baked them myself." She chuckled at her comment.

He didn't question her on the issue.

After he was seated, Karen rose and carried the album to his side. She slid onto the arm of his chair and set the album in his lap. "Tell me about these photographs. Who was this guy?" She pointed to a photo where her grandmother stood beside a young man who Karen knew wasn't her grandfather.

To her surprise, he flipped the album cover closed. "I don't remember all that fiddle-faddle. You should pitch those books in the trash. They're just sentimental things your grandmother hung on to. They don't mean anything to me."

Karen rose, stunned by his words. She lifted the album and cradled it in her arms. Maybe he didn't want to see the pictures, but she did. She loved wandering back in time and learning more about her grandparents.

Sensing her grandfather's moodiness, Karen slipped the photos back onto the shelf with the others and stood in front of the window. While she had spent away the time, the rain had stopped, and the sun had returned. The rainwater had already baked away, leaving a heavy weight of humidity suspended on the air. An occasional breeze rustled the leaves. Karen returned to the kitchen and slipped two more cookies onto her grease-stained napkin. She'd pay for the calories later, but now she was soothing her depression. She couldn't believe her grandfather's abrupt reaction to the album.

Karen looked through the back window and eyed the bench beneath the large oak in the backyard. The setting drew her forward, and she headed outside, trying to make sense out of what had happened.

No sooner had she sunk onto the bench, when she caught sight of Eric crossing his grandfather's lawn. He reached the fence, grasped the picket crossbars, and did a springing leap. He landed on both feet on her side of the fence. Neither her mind nor the fence served as a barrier to Eric's presence in her life. Her chest tightened as he neared her.

"Mind if I sit?" he asked, plopping beside her on the bench.

"No. Please. Have a seat." She gestured toward the spot he'd already sat on.

He laughed, then eyed the napkin in her lap. "Did you bake those?"

She looked down at the one lone cookie. "Yes, I baked them."

"I love chocolate chip," he said.

"Be my guest." She handed him the napkin, and he took it

without an argument. Before she could lower her hand, he'd consumed the whole cookie. A dusting of crumbs lay on his lip, and she longed to brush them away but controlled the urge.

Eric must have felt them. He used the paper napkin to wipe his mouth, then wadded it, and put it in his pocket. "Thanks. It was good."

She liked his smile and his easy way. So often life left her uptight and edgy, particularly her job, but Eric always had a genial manner and a quick wit. She liked that in a person. She liked it especially in Eric.

"Am I disturbing you?" he asked.

"No, I'm just sitting here."

"Doing nothing?"

"Right." In truth she was escaping her grandfather's mood. With the album coming to mind, she found herself wanting to talk about what happened. "I'm avoiding my grandfather right now."

"Really?" His eyebrows flew upward like two startled birds. She told him about the photograph album incident.

Eric's face registered a kaleidoscope of emotions as he gazed across the yard while she spoke as if he were miles away.

She wondered if he were listening. "I guess it was nostalgia, but I loved seeing my grandparents young again."

When she'd finished the story, he turned to her. "Why would he tell you to pitch the albums?"

"I don't know. He reacted almost as he does when your grandfather's name comes into the conversation. Just too strange."

"I don't understand either one of them," he said, rubbing the back of his neck.

Karen's heart felt heavy. "I wish I could do something about it. Arguments shouldn't last a lifetime."

"Maybe not, but I think this one will. I doubt if they'll ever change."

Karen shook her head. "Not true. Things can change. God

can do anything. The problem needs our prayer."

A look of interest spread across Eric's face. "You think so?"

She didn't know how to answer his curious question. "Yes," she said. "Don't you?"

She waited, but he didn't answer.

four

Karen woke with Eric on her mind. As they had sat in the backyard talking the day before, she felt comfortable and surprisingly amiable. Even though he was a member of her grandfather's "dreaded enemy's" family, she saw only his kindness and understanding, and she loved his wit. Even when she wanted to be angry at him and stick by her grandfather's side in his dispute with Lionel Kendall, Eric made her laugh.

Looking at the photographs yesterday, Karen had thought about her grandmother. She missed her these past months since she died. Her grandfather tried to cover his sadness, but once in a while his face confirmed the loneliness and grief he felt for his loss. The look made Karen's heart ache.

For some reason today, Karen recalled her grandmother's comments about the feud and the words sent a pinprick down her back. "Lionel Kendall's a poor loser," she'd said. Poor loser? Karen couldn't imagine the eternal feud being over winning or losing a football scrimmage or a game of checkers. Now that she recalled the comment, she wished her grandmother were there to explain.

In the quiet of the morning, Karen knelt by her bedside and asked God what she could do to end the foolish bickering between the two elderly men. One word entered her mind— patience. If the Lord had sent that word into her thoughts, she needed to explain. *Father, I'm not a patient woman. Please, Lord, give me some other way.* She felt her eyes well with tears as she said "amen." The task seemed so hopeless.

In the quiet of her room, Karen felt God's presence, and she sensed His guidance, but the exact action He wanted her to take seemed lost. She rose from the carpeted floor and sat on the edge of her bed. Her Bible lay on the bedside table where she'd left it the night before. She grasped it and turned the pages to the Gospel of Luke. Fingering the tissue-thin sheets, she scanned the verses while her eyes sought the message God wanted to share with her.

Karen stopped, letting the words sink into her mind. *But love your enemies, do good to them, and lend to them without expecting to get anything back. Then your reward will be great.* So simple. Love was the answer. Somehow she had to help her grandfather see that nothing was solved with anger and spite, but love was the answer. Yet how? Would her stubborn grandfather ever listen?

Lord, she reflected, closing her Bible, *thank You for the clear and simple message that can change the world. Please give me the patience I need. In Jesus' precious name. Amen.* She rose, straightened her knit top, and brushed off her jeans. Drawing her shoulders back, she headed through the bedroom doorway toward the kitchen. She needed resolve.

Before she stepped through the doorway, she smelled her grandfather's cooking—burnt toast and strong coffee. "What's for breakfast, Grandpa?" she asked, knowing full well she'd settle for milk and cereal.

"Made some fried eggs," he said.

His voice sounded thick in his throat, and she noticed a strained look on his face. Concern settled over her.

"You helpin' me this morning?" he asked, dropping his fork onto the empty plate.

"At the stand?"

He nodded. "Saturday's busy. I could use the help."

"You know I will." She gave his cheek a pat then kissed him over the spot, feeling an unnatural warmth on his face. "You're not feeling well, are you?"

He shrugged.

"You can't fool me, so stop trying. I think I inherited a keen eye from Grandma. She always knew when anyone was sick."

"It's just a summer cold. My chest feels tight, and my throat's scratchy."

"Then don't open the stand today," Karen said as she sprinkled some cereal into a bowl. "You should rest."

"An old man needs a purpose or else he gets sicker. I like talkin' to the customers, and I'm not sick. I'm just a little slow today."

Karen knew she'd get farther talking to the wall. She ate her breakfast with speed and drank her milk. She would have preferred a good cup of coffee, but the stuff her grandfather had brewed could disintegrate a spoon.

After she rinsed off the bowl, Karen hurried to the shed for the handcart. Yesterday they'd left the vegetables loaded on the dolly. Later in the day her grandfather had added some new produce, making the job easy this morning. She pushed the cart outside and headed toward the front yard, but before she reached the driveway, a bellow echoed from the house. Karen dropped the cart handle and dashed toward the noise.

"What's wrong?" she called, as she raced through the back doorway onto the porch.

"It's that scoundrel," he yelled from the front of the house. "He's parked his car in front of my stand."

Karen followed her grandfather's voice to the front door, and sure enough, Lionel Kendall's automobile was stationed on the gravel shoulder, blocking her grandfather's roadside stand.

"I'll sue the buzzard. He's a low down, dirty—"

"Grandpa, please. You're a Christian, and you know better. What does God say you should do when you're upset with a neighbor?"

"Park my car in front of his roadside stand—that is, if he had one."

She faltered at his comment. "That's not what God says." Her voice softened.

"Sure does. 'An eye for an eye. A tooth for a tooth.' So why not a parked car for a parked car?"

Karen shook her head. "Grandpa, you know why." She rested her hand on his shoulder. "Should I get my Bible?"

He lowered his gaze, and her heart softened. She sensed God's urging. Instead of huffing and puffing, she calmed herself and sat in the chair beside him. "An eye for an eye is in the Old Testament. When Jesus came to earth, He gave us some new commands to follow. I know you've read them. Jesus said, 'I know you've heard eye for eye and tooth for tooth,' but I tell you, Do not resist an evil person. If someone strikes you on the right cheek, turn to him the other also." Her grandfather shifted his gaze from the floor as if he wanted to counter her comment, but he couldn't debate with the Lord.

Karen stared at him until he looked at her. "And you know what else the Bible says?"

He shrugged.

"Love your enemy and pray for him."

She watched him bristle. "I can pray for him," he sputtered, "but I can't love him."

"Just try, Grandpa. Not for me, but for yourself." She gave him a hug and rose. "Just think about it. Don't do it for me. Do it for yourself."

Before he could come back with a comment, she turned and made her way through the front doorway. She'd kept control of her frustration in front of her grandfather, but as she marched across the Kendalls' front lawn, her irritation sparked. When she reached the neighbors' door, her hand folded into a fist, and she pounded on the frame until something pinged in her mind. Instead, she unfolded her hand and gave a final tap. *Patience and love,* she reminded herself.

The door opened, and Lionel Kendall stood facing her with a scowl on his face.

"Hi, Mr. Kendall," Karen said, forcing a pleasant grin. "I'm Walter Chapman's granddaughter, Karen. Remember me?"

He pursed his lips but otherwise didn't move.

"I noticed that you accidentally left your car in front of my grandfather's produce stand. I wonder if you'd mind moving it so we can open up this morning."

He still didn't say a word, but his eyes narrowed, and she could almost hear the thoughts grinding through his head.

"What's up?" Eric said, sliding in beside his grandfather.

Karen gave a wave toward the roadside stand. "We have a little problem."

Eric pushed open the screen door and leaned out. He looked toward heaven then gave Karen a knowing look. "Sorry, Karen. I'm sure my granddad wasn't thinking when he—"

"I was too think—"

Eric cut off Lionel's words as smooth as a warm knife to butter. "He was thinking he should move the car. Right, Granddad?" He held out his hand, palm up. "If you give me the car keys, I'll save you the trouble of putting on your shoes."

Karen hid her smile and backed away. Eric had handled the situation like a pro, and she realized for the first time he really felt as frustrated as she had been, but his laid-back style didn't always reflect his feelings.

She breathed a relieved sigh. If she would only ask herself what Jesus would do before she acted, she might respond more like a Christian should, but sometimes the very human side of her won out. She strutted across the lawn, knowing her grandfather would be happy with the car moved, and the day could proceed without any more problems.

At least, she prayed that was the case.

❧

Eric watched her bounce across the lawn and felt his pulse

give a twitch. She stirred his emotions. Why was he having feelings for this woman? He barely knew her. The thought hung in his head. That wasn't exactly correct. He had known her well when they were kids, and she still seemed very much the same—full of spunk and very caring. He saw it in the way she handled her grandfather. Firmly, but with love and concern. Not only was she beautiful, but Karen seemed intelligent, too. Her conversations were enjoyable, and she wasn't afraid to offer an opinion. He hated to admit it, but she had made a good point about the farmers' possible attitudes toward his market idea. He needed to give that some thought.

The hard part was she confused him. Eric sensed that she liked him. When she let down her guard, he could see it in her face and hear it in her voice, but she seemed to withdraw when he got too close. He wondered why. Was it him or the family feud? Could it be something else? Perhaps she was involved with someone.

Eric stepped outside with the car keys and treaded across the lawn. Karen had vanished around the side of the house. Even thinking of her made his chest tighten. He needed to monitor his feelings. He'd tried and it didn't seem to be working.

By the time he moved the car, Karen had arrived at the stand with a handcart loaded with produce. Eric took a step toward his grandparents' house then changed his mind. "Need some help?" he asked.

She shrugged and seemed distracted.

"Something wrong?"

"My grandfather's not feeling well. He insisted on coming out here, so the only way I got him to stay inside was to promise I'd do this myself. I'm just praying I can handle it."

"No need to pray for that," Eric said, pleased that he could finally do something helpful for her. She'd only asked for one thing, and he'd batted zero in dealing with his grandfather. "I'll stick around as long as I can."

She paused, studying him as a bunch of carrots hung suspended in the air. "Why?"

"Because I'm a nice guy?" He answered it as a question and followed the words with a toying grin.

"You really are. Thanks for the offer."

They worked side by side, and before the first car stopped, the vegetables and apples were in place, and the price cards had been taped to the table. Eric was surprised how many drivers pulled off the road and climbed out to check the produce. He became the cashier and helped bag, since Karen seemed to have a good grasp of the questions customers asked about the vegetables and apples. She knew the variety of tomatoes and could tell the buyer the hour they'd been picked.

When a lull came, Karen joined him in one of the canvas chairs. She leaned her head back and drew in a lengthy breath. "I don't know how Grandpa does this. It's a lot of work."

"He's been at it for years, I suppose."

Karen nodded. "I'm very worried about him. He really doesn't look well, but he won't let me call a doctor. When my mom and dad lived nearby, they'd occasionally come over and help during the busy season, but now that they've moved out of state and since Grandma died, Grandpa's alone too much."

"I'm sure he is since your grandmother's gone. How long has it been?"

"Nearly a year. She died too young. It's been difficult for him."

He agreed. Death was so final for the living and something humans couldn't control.

She'd paused a moment. "Keeping busy, at least, helps me not think about things."

Hearing her comment niggled his curiosity. "What kind of things?"

She gave him a look as if she wished she hadn't said anything.

"I've been at a sort of. . .well. . .crisis in my life, I guess."

Immediately he wondered if it was the same kind of crisis he'd faced. "You broke up with someone?"

Her eyes widened. "No. I'm having a job dilemma. I have a good job at a social service agency, but it's stressful and depressing. I'm an advocate for children, and we try to keep families together. We deal with health issues and domestic problems. You can guess that the odds are poor, and the troubles are continuous. I work with a family, and when things look good, another family arrives on my intake list who's in worse condition. It's never ending."

He couldn't imagine dealing with that day in and day out. "What do you want to do?"

Her gaze captured his. "That's the problem. I don't know. I love the work, in a way. I just wonder if it's the location. A big city has so many sad problems. I'd love to be where a little help can get someone on his feet and my efforts seem to accomplish something. Now I feel like a paper shuffler. Sometimes good ideas never get anywhere because of all the red tape."

"I know about red tape," he said. "The business world has more than its share."

"It does." She glanced at her watch then looked down the road in both directions. "I suppose I could close for a while. Grandpa always likes to have the stand open around the time work lets out so he can catch the stragglers. I have lots to do today, but I can't concentrate. I'm too worried about Grandpa." She gave him a smile. "But God will see me through."

As she began to gather up the produce, Eric joined her, pleased about her positive attitude and her strong faith. He wished his faith were as steadfast. He tended to be wishy-washy at times with his beliefs. He believed in God and salvation through Jesus, but he didn't demonstrate it the way he should, and he definitely wasn't comfortable talking to others about his faith, as Karen seemed able to do.

When they'd loaded the handcart, Eric stepped toward the handle. "Let me do that."

"I'll be fine," she said. "Thanks for your help this morning."

"Don't forget to let me know if you need me later."

"I will." She gave the cart a yank and dragged it up the gravel driveway.

Eric was happy to help her, but he sensed her drawing away again, and he didn't want to push his luck. If he tried too hard, he could envision her shying away like a young colt being saddled. She wanted no restraints, no reins.

Finally he turned away and headed home, wondering what he could do to change the way things were going. Karen's words struck him. Maybe he couldn't do this alone. Prayer. The possibility settled over him. The Bible said "ask and you shall receive." He remembered that much. Perhaps it was time to ask the Lord for direction.

While he was at it, he should probably tell the Lord what he really wanted to see happen.

five

Karen stood in the kitchen trying to select something for dinner. Her back ached, and she felt sunburned. A sound caught her attention. *Tap. Tap.* Karen heard it again and headed for the front door. When she answered, she felt her mouth gape open like a baby bird waiting for a worm.

"Eric. What—" She paused. Asking him what he was doing there would have been rude. "Hi. This is unexpected." She pointed to the kettle he held between two colorful potholders. "What's that?"

"Gramma Bea sent this over for your grandfather and you. I hope you haven't made dinner."

Karen laughed. "No, not by a long shot. What's in the kettle?" She pushed open the door.

"Gramma's homemade chicken soup. It's more like stew, it's so thick. She believes chicken soup is medicine," he said, stepping inside.

"It is. I've seen it work." She flagged him toward the kitchen. "Tell her thanks so much. I'm aching all over. This gardening business is for someone else, not me."

He chuckled and set the pot on the stove. When he lifted the lid, the rich scent of chicken and noodles filled the air, and Karen's stomach churned with hunger. "Care to join us?"

"I already ate, but I might stay and visit."

"Okay," she said. "Let me get my grandfather." He surprised her by his willingness to stay. She had assumed he'd get out of the house as fast as possible, but he'd decided to take his chances on her grandfather.

She left the kitchen, motioning him to have a seat. When she reached the living room, she stood in front of her grandfather's recliner and watched him sleep. Before she walked away, he opened one eye and peered at her. "Who's here?"

"Eric's grandmother sent over some homemade soup. Chicken. It smells wonderful. Do you feel like eating?"

"Not anything from that house. Lionel probably dropped arsenic in the broth."

"Grandpa. Please stop that. Mrs. Kendall sent the soup to you out of the goodness of her heart. Grandma always said chicken noodle soup put a person back on the road to health." She bent down and stared at him nose to nose. "And you need to get on that road." She leaned closer and kissed his cheek.

Her grandfather kissed hers back and then straightened. "Is he gone?"

"Who? Eric?"

He nodded.

"No. He's in the kitchen, waiting. Do you know he spent all morning with me working at the stand? He did it to help you."

"He did?" He lowered his gaze, and his mouth worked around the thought that was waiting to be spoken. "If that's the case, I guess he can stay."

She lifted her shoulders in frustration and gave her grandfather her hand to help him rise. She felt helpless and wondered what the Lord had in mind to heal the rift.

Walter tottered into the kitchen, using the wall and doorframes as support. Karen could see he really wasn't feeling well. Tomorrow morning she wasn't going to listen to his "no" response any longer. He was going to see a doctor unless he bounded out of bed wearing a pair of tap shoes.

Karen stepped into the kitchen behind her grandfather, and Eric rose, giving them a nod. "I hope you're feeling better, sir."

Her grandfather sniffed the air then let his gaze linger on the pot of soup. "Thank you. . .and for the soup, too. Tell your grandmother I appreciate it."

As they ate, Karen talked about the vegetables she picked earlier and the number of customers she had. Eric mainly listened, but occasionally, he added a comment about the problems farmers have selling their produce while fighting bad weather. Her grandfather warmed up, and soon he was acting more like himself with Eric. The picture filled Karen's heart as much as the soup and crackers filled her stomach.

After dinner, Walter decided to rest, and when the kitchen was cleaned and the rest of the soup refrigerated, Karen prepared a plate of cookies and poured glasses of iced tea before inviting Eric into the living room.

He followed and needed no invitation to take one of the cookies before he found a seat. "These are tasty."

Honesty nudged her. "They're the cut-and-bake kind. You can buy them in the dairy case."

"Really?" He picked up another and took a bite. "I thought you said you baked them yourself."

"I did. I just didn't prepare the dough."

He gave her a wink as if he already knew that and was only teasing her.

She relaxed and tucked her legs beneath her on the sofa. "I told you about myself earlier today. Tell me about you. What do you do for a living?"

He hesitated, and his reaction threw Karen a curve.

"I—I'm sort of between jobs," he said. He looked uncomfortable with his answer.

"Between jobs? Then you're unemployed." She didn't like that at all.

❧

Unemployed?

Eric swallowed and wanted to kick himself. He should have seen this coming. She told him all about herself earlier in the day, and he'd said nothing. He figured it was only natural for her to ask some question, but he didn't want to answer or explain. Not now.

"Not exactly," he said finally, "I'm looking into an investment."

"Investment? What kind?"

"Property," he said.

Her nose wrinkled. "I never thought of owning property as a business."

"It is when a person does something with it." He felt himself getting defensive. He just wished he could tell her the truth and get it over with, but she was way too opinionated for him to be that open. "I have plans for the property." He saw her question coming. "I'm still working on the project."

"Oh."

That was it. An empty response, but at least one that wasn't a challenge. He'd accept it for that. "I was working for an electronics firm. We made products that go into automotive electrical systems. I was a company representative. It was okay, but very unfulfilling. I prefer talking with customers who are buying the car, not a part to put in one. Much more rewarding. That's what I'm aiming for now."

Her face had softened, and her expression had grown tender. "I like hearing about you. You're excited about your new prospects."

He winced. "I don't like talking about myself. Maybe that's a man thing."

"Probably. Men don't want to show their emotions. It's nice to see you excited and protective about your new investment." Karen paused a moment, then straightened her legs and lowered them to the floor. She rested her elbow on her knees and propped her chin in her hands. "What about you? Do you have a special woman in your life?"

Her question caught him unaware, and he sucked in a breath in surprise. He'd been evasive about his work, but he couldn't do it now. Total honesty was important.

"I was seeing someone for a couple of years, but we broke it off recently."

A look of concern settled on her face. "I'm sorry, Eric."

"Don't be. I ended it." When the words came out, he knew it might have been the wrong thing to say. Her concern shifted to a frown. "It was better for us both."

"Really."

That was all she said. Eric wondered what it meant. Really, she didn't believe him or really, it was the best for them both. He didn't want to challenge her one-word comment, but he felt what he'd said needed an explanation. He tried to reveal why he'd decided to end the relationship. The more he talked, the feebler he sounded, almost as if he were looking for excuses. He hadn't been. Eric knew in his heart it was the right thing to do.

Karen looked at her watch, and Eric realized he was digging himself in deeper with every minute. "It's getting late," he said. "I'd better go."

She didn't stop him but rose and headed for the kitchen. "I'll get your grandmother's soup kettle."

When she returned, she handed it to him with a distant look in her eyes. "Tell your grandma thanks for the soup. It was delicious."

"I will," he said, stepping toward the door. "I hope I didn't bore you with all my talk. I shouldn't have said anything."

She placed her hand on his arm. "No. I'm glad you did."

She pushed open the screen, and he stepped out into the summer evening.

As Eric walked away his stomach tightened, wondering if he'd lost all chances now of getting to know Karen better. He'd hoped something special might develop between them. Tonight he doubted if she'd even consider being his friend.

❧

Sunday morning Karen was relieved to see Grandpa Walter's

surprising recovery. They laughed over whether or not it really was the chicken soup that brought him back to health. The next day her grandfather decided to leave the stand closed in the morning. Karen used the free time to look at the eaves troughs. She dragged a long extension ladder to the porch roof, and as she feared, they were clogged with debris. When she climbed down and stepped back, reality caught her by the throat. The house was two stories. She'd been okay on the ladder one story up, but two? She shook her head. Hiring someone made more sense. Still she wasn't sure her grandfather had that kind of money to waste.

After she brought out a large trash bag, Karen climbed the ladder again. She tied the bag to a top rung and began dragging out the mucky compost that had congested in the trough. Her mind drifted, as it always did, to Eric. He'd disappointed her yesterday with his two bits of news—unemployed and fresh from a romantic breakup. Karen didn't see him as a saint, but she'd sensed he had two feet placed tightly to the ground. She'd apparently been very mistaken, and that changed everything.

She paused a moment, looking at the rotting mess in the eaves and realizing that sometimes her behavior was as black and disgusting. She pushed her confused thoughts aside and returned to the job at hand. Digging her fingers in deeply, she pulled out a glob of waste and felt a splash of the black goop hit her cheek. With no free hand to wipe it off, she left it there.

No longer able to reach the debris in either direction, Karen realized she had to climb down to move the ladder.

Part way down the rungs, Eric's voice rose up to meet her. "What in the world are you doing?"

"Not having my tires rotated," she said, gazing down at him. She knew from his expression he recalled his exact comment in the grocery store days earlier.

"Okay. You got me," he said. Playfully, he hung his head, as if he was ashamed.

She continued down while he waited. As she shifted the ladder, he took it from her and moved it down a few feet, then turned to face her. "Nice decoration."

"What?"

"That glob on your face."

She lifted her clean hand and brushed away the slime. "I don't expect you to help me."

"I know that. I want to."

Karen lifted her chin, trying to keep her emotions from getting in the way of good sense. "I need to be honest, Eric. After talking last night, I really think that—"

"I'm sorry about last night. I know I sounded like an unemployed womanizer, but that's not true. Please trust me. When you get to know me better, you'll see who I am. Don't think I'm a bad guy because my grandfather's a little gruff."

She bit back her desire to question his "a little gruff" comment, then had second thoughts. The look on Eric's face and the sincerity in his eyes made her remember God's Word. "Do not judge, or you too will be judged." She hadn't given Eric or his grandfather a chance. "Why should I trust you?"

"Because I'm trustable." He grinned at his made-up word. "I've done nothing to make you think otherwise."

Shame covered her. "You're right, Eric. You've been nothing but helpful and kind. I'm sorry."

"Glad that's settled," he said. "Now let me get to work." He shifted the ladder, extended it its full length, then grasped the rungs, and headed to the second-story eaves.

Karen watched as he climbed to the top without a qualm. Her knees would be knocking as they were now just watching him. She clung to the ladder rails to support it and waited, praying he wouldn't break his neck. Karen wanted to do that herself if she found out he wasn't telling her the truth.

～

Karen scrutinized her grandfather raking broken limbs and dried grass into a pile in the backyard. Another rainstorm had hit in the night, and branches lay strewn across the lawn. Karen had suggested he wait a day or two. The wind was still whipping the leaves, and raking seemed a futile task, but her grandfather had gone out anyway. Now Karen felt guilty, watching him.

As useless as the job seemed to be, she left the back porch with the hope she could help him finish the task before he got sick again. "Grandpa, the wind's shifting things around today. It's hopeless. Let's wait until tomorrow."

"It's almost finished," he said, as determined as ever.

"You should have put this farther back, don't you think?"

"This is a good spot. No trees to catch fire."

"Catch fire?" Karen looked at him, then at the pile he'd assembled very close to the Kendalls' fence. "You can't burn this here, Grandpa. You'll start the fence on fire."

"No, I'll watch it," he said.

Before she could stop him, he knelt down and dropped a lit match into the limbs. Dried grass smoldered then spread, and soon the limbs were snapping and sending firefly sparks into the air. Karen watched with dismay as the dark smoke curled upward, then sailed across the fence into the Kendalls' yard, where Lionel was sitting beneath a tree with the daily newspaper.

"I should have known," she said, marching across the grass toward the water hose.

"No, you don't," her grandfather called.

"Yes, I do, and please move out of the way or you'll get wet."

Lionel Kendall was hanging over the fence, shaking his fist, while her grandfather made faces at him like a child.

Lord, help me, Karen pleaded. She cranked on the water spigot and headed toward the flames. As she neared, she turned on the water nozzle, and both men backed up as she aimed the stream at the fire.

Her grandfather strode away, grumbling under his breath, but Mr. Kendall clung to the pickets, still shaking his fist. In a heartbeat Eric came to her rescue. He guided his grandfather back to the chair, returned to the fence, propelled another daring leap, and landed on her side of the barrier.

"Two little kids," Eric said. He walked toward her with his fingers planted in his jeans pockets.

"I'm sorry about this. I'd hoped my grandfather could learn to turn the other cheek."

"You're looking for a miracle," he said, chuckling.

Karen didn't like his laughing at her comment. She was serious. She couldn't work a miracle, but God could, and she'd hoped the Lord might provide it.

"Let me help." He tugged his fingers from beneath the denim and grabbed the rake.

She was too tired and frustrated to argue.

six

The breeze rustled the leaves of the huge oak tree in the back woods. The rough bark scuffed against Karen's jeans as she sat on the broad limb and surrendered herself to the quiet and to God's voice. She'd been fighting the desires of her heart, and she wasn't sure if the warning voice she heard was the Lord's or her own worries.

Karen knew better than to link herself with an unbeliever. She'd been wanting to talk to Eric about his faith, but part of her was too afraid to hear the truth. If he confessed he wasn't a Christian, she would have to walk away, so not knowing seemed easier. Yet she knew she was leading herself into temptation. She asked God's forgiveness and strength to do what was right.

No matter how Eric might answer her question, Karen had to admit he reflected many gifts of the spirit. He'd been thoughtful so many times—helping at the stand, cleaning the eaves troughs, coming to her aid with the rubbish fire issue, too many things to list. He'd been compassionate. He'd shown concern over her grandfather's health and showed the same with her job problems and other concerns. Eric loved his family, another important attribute in Karen's eyes. He also gave her the gift of laughter. So many times, when she wanted to be angry, Eric smoothed out her ire by bringing a smile to her face. But Karen wasn't fooled. Unbelievers could show the same attributes. Thoughtfulness and kindness were no guarantee. Still, she enjoyed his company. More than enjoyed it, if she were to be truthful to herself.

The sun sprinkled a patter of speckled light along the path

below and made the tree leaves shimmer with its glow, outlining the veins and shapes. Even more had changed to autumn hues. Gold and red dominated the once-green foliage, reminding her that summer was fading and her vacation as well. She'd return to her job and the stress she so disliked.

Maybe she should quit. The words popped into her thoughts and out again in a heartbeat. Karen liked to plan ahead, to know where she was going. Perhaps that's why Eric's admission that he was between jobs set her on edge. She couldn't imagine being jobless, but was being between jobs really so bad?

Lately she'd neglected prayers for herself. Worried about her grandfather, Karen's prayers had been focused on him and on her concerns for Eric, but her employment needed prayer as well. Karen closed her eyes and spoke to the Lord from her heart, and when she said "amen," a calm washed over her like spring sunshine. Her heart warmed, and she knew that God was in charge.

Karen began to hum. Then the words filled her mind. *Amazing Grace.* The Lord saved wretches like her and like so many who walked the earth. How precious was God's grace and love. She felt it shimmer on the summer breeze like a balm.

"Hello, songbird."

Eric's voice made her pulse skip.

"Caught me again." He looked so handsome and refreshing. So often he'd become her spring rain, sprinkling her with drops of humor and reflection. . .and sometimes ruining her picnic, but that was life. If he didn't rile her a bit, she would wonder if perhaps he wasn't a real friend.

"I'm enjoying the solitude," she said from above him.

"Solitude?" He pinched his chin, as if in thought. "Does that mean you're enjoying being alone or being quiet?"

She couldn't help grinning at his question. "Just enjoying."

"Are you coming down, or should I come up?"

Karen had no plans to come down just yet, but she wasn't sure she wanted him in the tree beside her. "If you promise to be quiet." The words slipped out unbidden.

"I can't promise that," he said, grasping a lower limb and boosting himself upward until he settled on a nearby branch. "It's nice up here," he said, his voice breathless from his climb. "No wonder you sit in tree branches. I haven't done this since I was a boy."

She leaned against the trunk. "It is nice and peaceful. You shouldn't let life pass you by. As they say, take time to smell the—"

"You mean take time to climb the trees, don't you?"

"That, too," she said.

Silence settled over them. Only the sounds of the woods—bird calls, whispering leaves, and chirping insects—broke the hush.

"Please don't stop singing. That's what drew me here." His comment interrupted the quiet.

A little uncomfortable at having an audience, she ignored his request, but soon the song hung in her serene thoughts, and she continued the song she'd begun earlier. When she finished the last verse, a ray of sunlight broke through the canopy of trees and fell on her. She narrowed her eyes to keep out the bright light.

"A spotlight for the performer," Eric said, offering his applause.

She shushed him, uneasy with his accolades. She was singing to God, not to Eric.

"Everything's been civil for the past couple days," he said.

"Civil?"

"With our grandfathers. They haven't tried to maim or destroy one another's property. I'm saying that's progress." He sent her an invigorating smile.

"You're right. Good things can happen with time." *And patience,* she added to herself. Her words were a good reminder. "Anything new in your life?"

"My, um, job offer looks good. I should know what's happening very soon."

His comment surprised her. The last she knew, he was between jobs. "You didn't mention you had an application in for a job."

"You didn't ask me."

True. She hadn't, but. . .

"I don't want to talk about it yet until I'm confident everything's going as I hoped. It's embarrassing to announce a. . .new job and then lose it."

Karen's heart lifted. "I understand." One negative concern had sailed away. He wasn't just a loafer. She cringed with the admission. She knew he wasn't a goof-off already. No matter what he said about himself, Eric had worked hard since she'd met him, and mainly for her and her grandfather. How could she doubt he was enterprising?

As she shifted, Karen's branch gave a groaning creak. Fearing it might break, she clutched at the trunk. "I'd better get off of this before I go down the quick way."

"Right now you're out on a limb, literally," he said, grinning at her, "but I think it's just the old oak's growing pains. Still you shouldn't take chances."

Eric shifted from his branch to get out of her way and lowered his foot to feel the limb below. Karen followed, moving from branch to branch, with Eric below her. When he reached the ground, he raised his arms, grabbed her by the waist, and swung her down from the final limb. He lowered her to the ground, where they stood face-to-face.

Her heart gave a wild thump, and her blood raced through her body as she faced the truth. She wanted Eric to kiss her. Searching his eyes, she saw the same look reflected in his, but too many issues still clung to her reasoning. Harnessing her emotions, she stepped back and won the battle. Still her lips could almost feel the soft, sweet touch of Eric's.

He cleared his throat, tucked his fingers into his jeans as if to tether them, and took a step down the path. Eric waited until she followed. They walked side by side, hands brushing against each other as they went. When they came out of the woods, they crossed a meadow into the apple orchard. Eric stopped long enough to pick two apples from a tree. He polished them on his shirt and threw a shiny orb to Karen. She caught it. Together they bit into the juicy pulp. No words were spoken, but the silence seemed to speak as they headed back to their houses.

Eric said good-bye when they reached the garden. Karen watched his broad shoulders sway with each step. If only he were less evasive, she would feel less confused. As she made her way toward the house, she realized her grandfather was in the garden, picking vegetables. As she neared, he straightened and gave her a look.

"You with that Kendall guy again?" he asked.

She bent down to pluck a ripe tomato from its stem. "His name's Eric. I ran into him in the woods."

"He seems to hang around the woods a lot, wouldn't you say?"

She placed the tomato into the basket sitting beside her grandfather's feet. "I wouldn't call it hanging around. He was passing through and heard me singing."

Her grandfather motioned toward the distant trees. "Why are you singing out there? Singing's for church."

"It's for anyplace the spirit moves me, Grandpa." Teasing, she patted his head. "Don't get yourself in a tizzy, please. Eric's a nice man."

"He's probably a heathen like the rest of them. Lionel raised all his boys that way."

"Are you sure, or are you speculating?"

He gave his shoulder a shrug. "Just makes sense."

"Not to me," Karen said. "Eric's his grandson. A lot of things could have brought him to know the Lord." She said the words but wondered how true her words were.

"An apple doesn't fall too far from the tree. Ever hear that?"

She had, but she wanted to give Eric a chance.

"I'm busy now." Walter crouched down and began gathering the rosy, warm tomatoes for the basket.

Feeling suddenly disappointed, Karen turned her back and walked toward the house. She should have asked him when they were in the woods. Then instead of wondering and worrying, she'd know the truth.

❧

Eric slid from his automobile and climbed the steps of My Friend's Place. He'd volunteered to help paint some of the rooms, a volunteer project his grandmother's church was supporting. He smiled at the organization's name. A home for abused women and families, My Friend's Place had a genial sound and gave the families who came there a welcome feeling. "I'm staying at my friend's place," they could say, without feeling uneasy.

He tapped on the door, and another church member, Bill Jackson, invited him in. He looked around, surprised to see the rooms without occupants.

"All of the families are on a picnic while we paint," Bill said, apparently noticing Eric's curious expression. "It protects their identity. Some are nervous around men, so they try to go somewhere when we come in to do maintenance."

"Good idea."

"Although I've come by to help with plumbing and they've stayed," Bill said. "With painting, I suppose it's easier for them to spend the day away."

Eric followed Bill through the house, noticing the small bedrooms, some with evidence of young children by the clutter of coloring books or building blocks. His heart ached, knowing that within these walls, women and children had to find refuge from an abusive spouse.

His life wasn't perfect, but he'd come from a loving home. Not much religion came through his door. His father cursed and drank, but he was kind in his own way. Eric had been encouraged in his faith by his grandmother Bea. She'd not been regular at worship, but she'd taught him stories about Jesus, and he followed her examples of kindness and gentleness. He found it hard to believe that some of that sweetness didn't rub off on his grandfather. Eric supposed much of his grandfather's gruffness was for effect and that deep inside he was a loving man who didn't know how to break away from his reputation.

Bill set him up with brushes, rollers, tape, and a gallon of paint, and Eric got busy. He moved the furniture to the center of the room and covered it with plastic sheets, but before he did, he'd notice a small family photo on the dresser. A slender, tired-looking woman with two children, a boy and girl of elementary school age, he figured.

Eric thanked God for My Friend's Place, but he didn't think it was the best home for children. He knew they were basically confined to the small house and narrow yard—no place to run or play ball, little to stimulate their minds but a couple televisions he'd noticed in the common rooms. If he could only make a difference in a few lives, his purpose would be worthwhile.

❧

Eric seemed to have vanished for a couple of days. Karen missed his unexpected visits and silly grin. She hadn't laughed since she'd last seen him. She disliked the disappointment that she felt and knew that he shouldn't mean so much to her. Soon they would be going their separate ways, and then what?

She dressed quickly and headed down to breakfast. If she

didn't hurry, they'd be late for Sunday worship. The service began at eight A.M., probably leftover from an older generation of early risers.

"You look handsome, Grandpa," Karen said, admiring his short-sleeved dress shirt and pressed trousers. His sunbrowned arms showed beneath the sleeve hems, giving him a healthy glow.

"You look mighty pretty yourself," he said, wrapping his arm around her shoulder. "Sometimes you remind me of your grandma. She was a strong spunky woman, too."

His image of Karen caused her to chuckle. Maybe she was strong and spunky. She'd never thought of herself like that.

She drove her grandfather to church, preferring to get there relaxed and not on edge, as she felt with her grandfather's aggressive driving. The church parking lot was half full, and the sight disappointed her. Then she remembered summer. People traveled, as she was doing. Her hidden longing was to walk into the sanctuary and see Eric sitting there alone, perhaps, or with his grandmother. Karen recalled Gramma Bea was a Christian woman. Perhaps her faith rubbed off on Eric.

Once inside, she saw that her secret dream wasn't fulfilled. Eric's dark wavy hair and playful smile weren't there.

They settled into what she'd gotten to know as her grandfather's pew. He sat in the same place each Sunday, as if his name were on the bench. It wasn't. She'd even checked once—on both sides—just to make sure, but she had noticed since she'd attended church with her grandfather that many people sat in the same seats.

The service began, and her voice lifted in song while her grandfather's deep-throated mumble sounded beside her. Though his voice wasn't melodic, his spirit was, and that's what counted. They sat for the choir's musical selection and the readings. While she leaned against the pew, her thoughts drifted again to Eric as they so often did. She compared her yearning to a child with a nickel looking into a candy store where everything cost a dime. The looking was useless, and she'd make more progress going somewhere else to spend her five cents.

On the cover of the morning's program was a picture of a vine growing from a stem and winding around a tree, much like one of the large oak trees in the woods. The lesson focused on Jesus as the vine and believers as the branches. The words took her back to her grandfather's garden. She could see the cucumber plants winding their way along the ground, heading in many directions, all from one stem. The pastor's voice rang through the large sanctuary reading from John's Gospel. The words captured Karen's thoughts.

" 'Remain in me, and I will remain in you,' " the pastor said. " 'No branch can bear fruit by itself; it must remain in the vine. Neither can you bear fruit unless you remain in me.' "

Had she stayed in the vine, or had she strayed? In the past days, she'd borne no fruit as far as her grandfather's situation. "No branch can bear fruit by itself; it must remain in the vine. Neither can you bear fruit unless you remain in me." Had this been the reason for her failure? Had she again tried to solve the problem on her own without the Lord's blessing? She'd been out on a limb by herself, disjointed and not connected to the Lord. She needed to cling to the branches of her faith when it came to her grandfather's troubles, her feelings about Eric, and her job indecision. Prayer and God's Word were the way. She'd said it so many times, but too often she spoke the prayer without really connecting to the Vine.

The awareness left her heavy with thought, and when the congregation rose to sing the last hymn, she remained seated until her grandfather touched her arm. Embarrassed at her distraction, Karen rose and grabbed the songbook.

Outside, she stood in the morning sun, waiting for her

grandfather, and her thoughts became prayers. Today, she felt connected, and later, when the time seemed right, she hoped to help her grandfather see the analogy of bearing good fruit in his relationship to Lionel Kendall. If nothing more happened this summer, she prayed God would help her make a difference.

seven

Karen sat on the back porch after church. Her gaze drifted every few minutes to the Kendall yard. She still hadn't seen Eric, and she'd begun to wonder if he'd gone back home without saying good-bye. Loneliness washed over her—a feeling she wanted to escape.

Solitude had never bothered Karen. She'd lived with it for a long time, not because she didn't like to be around people and not because she was afraid to date, but because she felt weighted by her work. She found it difficult to come home to her comfortable apartment and look forward to a life of luxury and social events when daily she saw people who didn't even have the necessities.

With those feelings knotted inside her, Karen gave her all at work, but her all didn't seem to be enough. Now she'd run into another wall. She'd met a man who touched her heart and made her laugh, but it would end there. Instead of mourning over what wasn't, Karen thought about what was. God had given her a few bright days and many cheerful moments. Laughter was good for the heart and soul. She could handle whatever the Lord had in mind for her. Her sacrifice was so small compared to God's gift of His Son, who died for her sins. Her own earthly wants seemed so unimportant.

She drew up her shoulders and headed inside. Dinnertime was coming quickly, and she needed to make decisions. When she reached the living room, she drew up short. Her grandfather sat in his recliner, his gaze directed out the window, his eyes misted, and Karen's heart weighted with his sadness.

Not wanting to interfere, she took a step backward, but he'd noticed her and sat up straighter.

"Are you getting hungry, Grandpa?" Karen asked.

"A little, I suppose."

She walked across the room and sat on the arm of his chair. "Something bothering you?"

He waved away her words. "Just an old man being melancholy."

She placed her hand against his arm. "Thinking of Grandma?"

He tilted his head toward hers. "Always."

Karen wanted to cry. She missed her grandmother, too, but she had no comprehension of how much he missed her, the married couple having spent so many years together day after day. "Anything I can do?"

He pressed his lips together and shook his head. "Not unless you want to organize a pie booth." His sadness melted behind a half smile.

"A pie booth?"

"For the Arts and Apple Fest. The city has one every year, and your grandma always rallied the ladies together from the church and in the neighborhood to set up an apple pie booth."

"For what? The church?"

"No. They selected a local charity each year, and the proceeds went to benefit those who needed help." He leaned back against the chair and stretched out his legs. "Your grandma had a knack for finding the perfect charity that would get the women excited."

"And she made the best apple pies," Karen added.

"She did that, too."

Karen tensed as the thoughts ran through her mind. She was good at rallying people together, and though she didn't know the community well, she could probably locate the perfect charity, but if she had to bake pies, she'd destroy the fund-raiser. Pies and Karen were like oil and water. They didn't mix.

"Let me think on it, Grandpa," she said after a moment's silence. "Maybe I can help. No promises now, but I'll mull it over in my mind and see what I can do."

"You'd do that for me?" His voice lifted with the words.

"For you and Grandma. . .and the charity."

"You're a sweet woman, Karen. Your grandmother would be proud of you."

Karen wanted to stop him. She hadn't said yes yet.

Or had she?

ठ

Flour sprinkled the countertop and floor as Karen rolled out a piecrust. If she could handle the pie-making part of the requirement, she would volunteer to do this project that was so important to her grandfather. She feared she'd already volunteered in his eyes.

She winced, eyeing the crust recipe, but gathered courage and followed directions. Making a pie couldn't be that difficult. She had called Eric's grandmother for a recipe, and the older woman offered to do an honest taste test when it was finished. Karen was anxious to go for a visit, since she learned that Eric had not left town but had gotten involved in a volunteer project of some kind. She was curious what that was all about.

After the ingredients were arranged on the kitchen counter, Karen mixed the dough, formed a firm ball, then grasped the wooden rolling pin and began the processes of flattening the dough. She smiled as it spread into a thin circle. But her smile faded when the crust clung to the wooden cylinder as she tried to lift it. A ragged hole gaped in the middle of the perfect circle.

She balled up the dough, kneaded it back together, and

began again, but this time her heart sank when the pie dough adhered to the countertop. Trying to keep a positive attitude, she scraped it up and pressed the dough together. Then, using a mass of flour, Karen found success. She lifted the round shape and plopped it into the pie tin, breathing a deep sigh, which sent a gust of flour dust into the air. She waved it away with her equally white hands.

Feeling more confident now, she began the filling. She peeled the apples then added the flour and sugar. She opened the spice cupboard and saw a jar of cinnamon, but no nutmeg. Doubling the cinnamon would do, she decided, and she added two measured scoops. She spread the mixture into the piecrust and added a few pats of butter, and a crumbly streusel topping finished it off before she popped it into the oven.

The sweet scent filled the air, as pride filled her chest. The pie smelled sweet and tangy, if nothing else, and she couldn't wait to take it next door. When it came from the oven, she almost took a sample taste, but the golden crust looked so inviting, she decided to take it next door uncut.

Karen freshened up, then carried the still-warm pie across the grass and knocked on Gramma Bea's door. Her heart rose to her throat, hoping that Eric would answer, but instead, his grandmother stood before her when the door had opened.

"Mercy," she said with a flicker of amusement in her eye, "what do you have here?"

"Apple pie," she said. "You offered to taste test, and here I am."

Gramma Bea pushed open the screen and stepped back. Karen came through, her picture-perfect pie held between two potholders. The woman beckoned her to follow, and they passed through the dining room into the kitchen.

Karen kept her eyes moving like a searchlight, fearing Eric's grandfather would burst on the scene and scare her with one of his booming comments. She could imagine her pie in crumbles on the floor, but he didn't appear. Neither did Eric, to her disappointment.

"Let me have a taste of this," Gramma Bea said, as she dug into a drawer. She pulled out a wedge-shaped utensil with a serrated edge and made a slice, then another, and placed them on saucers. "Here's one for you." She handed Karen the plate.

Karen watched, holding her breath. The older woman produced two forks from another drawer, but before they dug in, Eric came through the doorway.

Karen faltered and lowered her fork.

"This is a surprise," he said.

Gramma Bea's hand stood suspended as well. She lowered it and headed for another plate and fork. "I suppose you want to try Karen's first apple pie."

He gave Karen an amused smile. "Your first. I can't believe it."

"I've never been much of a pie baker, but Grandpa asked me—not accurate—he *hinted* that he wished someone would take over my grandmother's involvement with the Arts and Apple Fest booth for charity. I opened my mouth."

"Good for you," Eric said.

He accepted the pie from his grandmother and dug in. His face took on a look of surprise, and Karen didn't know if the surprise was he didn't expect her pie to be so good or it was a disaster.

Karen lifted the fork to her lips as Gramma Bea made a choking sound. Karen slipped a piece into her mouth and felt her heart sink to the basement. She longed to spit out the contents, but that wasn't ladylike or polite. "It's awful," she moaned. "What did I do?"

Eric had finally swallowed and set the pie onto the table. "I don't know, but it's hot as fire, and the taste isn't cinnamon."

"It's chili powder," Gramma Bea said. "The jars look alike. I think you picked up the wrong spice."

Chili pepper. She remembered seeing it beside the cinnamon,

and she'd thought to herself they looked somewhat alike. She could only imagine that not having the nutmeg threw her off. And her crust was like a rock. Embarrassment washed over her, and now she wished Eric hadn't appeared as she prayed he would. That was one plea she wished God had ignored.

"Maybe you should buy your spices in cans," Eric said. "You'll have to read the label and not just look at it."

"Hush," Gramma Bea said.

Karen ignored his comment, but inside she smiled. He was right. Reading the label would have helped. . .except for the piecrust. "Why is my crust so horrible?" she asked, facing that she might as well admit the total disaster.

"Overworked, I'd guess," Gramma Bea said. "The less handling the more tender the crust."

Karen remembered how many times she'd kneaded the dough back into a ball. Overhandling was right. "I'm mortified. . .and it looked so pretty."

"You get one point for pretty," Eric said, sending her a teasing look. "I have to admit the pie was different."

His grandmother gave him a playful swat. "Let the poor girl alone. She did her best."

"I hope that's not her best," Eric said, sputtering a laugh.

Karen opened her mouth to respond, but Gramma Bea beat her to it.

"She'll be the best pie maker in town once I get done with her. You can volunteer to organize the booth, Karen. I'll be happy to help in any way I can."

"I guess the first way is to help me learn to make a pie." The horrible taste still clung to Karen's tongue, and she was sure they were all being polite. "Could I have some water to wash this taste out of my mouth?"

Gramma Bea grinned. "How about some iced tea and some homemade cookies?"

"That sounds even better," Karen said.

"Count me in, too." Eric pulled out a kitchen chair and motioned Karen to have a seat.

She did, and he joined her while Gramma Bea poured the drinks and piled a plate full of goodies. The conversation dwindled while they nibbled. Karen knew the flurry of activity was motivated by her horrible pie. Finally they slowed and settled back to include conversation.

When the talk turned back to the Arts and Apple Fest, Karen brought up her next concern. "I need a charity. I really don't know the needs of the community here, and I know Grandma always had some specific purpose in mind. Any ideas?"

Gramma Bea pursed her lips in thought, but Eric jumped in immediately. "My Friend's Place would be a good choice."

Karen felt her forehead wrinkle. What did his friend's place have to do with a charity? "I don't understand."

Eric laughed. "I suppose that sounded strange. It's a safe haven for abused women and families. They call it My Friend's Place. I've been painting over there the past few days. Volunteers do most maintenance and repairs. The house has been open for a couple of years but hasn't had a lot of backing."

"My Friend's Place," Karen said. "I didn't think in a small community like Gaylord they would need a safe haven."

"Small communities can be the worst. Social life is limited unless a family is church active, and even then, people look for amusements, especially men. The local bar seems to fill their needs. They have a drink and shoot the breeze, then one drink leads to another, and you know where it goes from there."

Karen nodded. "I see so much of that in the city." The whole situation filled her with sadness. "The children break my heart. They're the innocent victims of most family problems."

"I promised to drive back to the shelter with another

gallon of paint so they can finish up bright and early tomorrow. If you'd like to ride along today and talk with the director, you're welcome to join me."

She paused a moment, as if uncertain. Eric saw the struggle reflected in her expression. He wondered why.

"Thanks. I think I will," she said, finally. "What time are you going?"

"I'll have lunch now, then go back. How about one-thirty?"

"Sounds good." She cringed, looking at the sample she'd brought over for Gramma Bea to try. "Guess I'd better get my booby-prize pie home and get ready. I'm still covered with flour dust."

"But it looks good on you," Eric said.

"Don't be dismayed, Karen," Gramma Bea said. "We can have our pie-making lesson whenever you're ready. I learned to make them from my grandmother."

Karen's emotions shifted to an ambiguous blend of joyful and sadness. "Wish I could say the same. Grandma made exceptional pies. I never bothered to learn."

"God's giving you a second chance," Gramma Bea said.

Her spirit lifted. "Second chances are great. Sometimes thirds are needed, but let's hope I get a home run on the next try."

ஃ

Eric couldn't help but smile as he ate his lunch. He recalled Karen's "one shoe on and one shoe off" embarrassment the day they met in the woods for the first time in years, and today she was even more humiliated with the pie. It was horrible. The taste returned to his memory, and he pushed it away. Chili powder had no place in an apple pie.

Pleasure filled him, knowing that Karen had agreed to visit the facility with him. She'd been rather standoffish, in a way, and he'd decided to do the painting project to give her time to stew over his absence. He guessed it worked, because it didn't take her too long to agree to go.

They hadn't discussed the family feud lately, and maybe that was the problem. Perhaps she thought he'd given up or figured he didn't care enough to do anything. He'd tried the best he could. He knew his grandfather and his stubborn nature. Pushing only doubled the problem, and being subtle didn't work either. He needed something in between.

If it wasn't the feud, then he didn't know what it was that kept her at a distance. She said she had no special male friend. He had to believe it was true. Why would she not admit it if she did have someone in her life?

He so longed to tell her about his bid on the property for his market. Only one issue needed to be resolved before the land and building was his. He planned to start small, but if it took off, he could add to the building, expand the stock. His thoughts filled with possibilities. Best of all, he'd be living right back here near his grandparents in northern Michigan farmland, the place he loved.

eight

Karen was ready when Eric pulled into the driveway. My Friend's Place filled the conversation as he drove her to the facility. He told her he'd called ahead, and the director welcomed her to visit, especially when she heard it involved a possible fund-raiser.

When they parked in front, Eric leaped from the car to open Karen's door. She waited and grinned when she let him be a gentleman. She looked at the house with interest. It was an older farmhouse, not far from the center of town. Like many farms, property sold off to investors, and little by little, the city grew up around once-fertile fields.

Karen stood a moment and studied the wide front porch. At first she wondered why it was empty and not filled with rocking chairs and benches. Then she remembered.

"I suppose they can't sit out front."

"Right," he said. "The back has a few trees and tall shrubs as well as a privacy fence around the small patio. It's not the greatest place for kids. It is safer, though, than when they were living at home."

Karen's jaw tightened as she nodded. He guided her up the sidewalk and rang the bell. The director opened the door.

"Welcome," she said. "You must be Karen. I'm Nadine Smith, the director of My Friend's Place."

"Thanks for letting me visit," Karen said.

"I hear you're thinking about doing a fund-raiser this year during the Arts and Apple Fest."

"My grandmother did this kind of thing for years, and she died almost a year ago. . .so I'm trying to fill in for her."

She gestured toward Eric. "Eric mentioned that you have quite a need here, and I thought I'd drop by and talk to you in person."

Eric touched Karen's arm and lifted the gallon of paint. "I'll take this to the basement while you look around."

Karen nodded and watched him go, then turned her attention to Nadine. The woman described the facility and its program, then listed its needs. As she listened, Karen had no doubt the haven for women and children was a worthy benevolence.

She viewed the empty bedrooms, but in the community room, women sat around talking or reading. Then Karen and Nadine came to a parlor turned into an indoor playroom. Inside, one of the women sat at a card table working on a puzzle with her children, a girl Karen figured was about eight and a boy. She guessed he was about nine or ten. The children were pale skinned, and Karen could only believe that sunshine and outdoor play would be a special treat for the boys and girls living here.

The woman looked up and gave a hesitant smile, but Karen saw the sadness in her eyes. The children wiggled in their chairs, as if eager to run free. But where?

Outside, Karen viewed the play area, a small section blocked from view by a privacy fence.

"We have to be so careful with the children. It's important that we shield them from danger or retribution of an angry father. Outdoor play has to be restricted. We even bus them to a different setting for school once it begins. It's impossible to let them attend their home schools."

Karen understood. She'd had a taste of this kind of problem in Detroit. "How could more funds add to the play area?"

"Perhaps you didn't notice, but the lot next door is for sale. We would love to extend a more secure privacy fence, add playground equipment, a slab for basketball, whatever we could fit in the area. We could make the patio area larger with a covered roof, so that in rain or hot sun, the women could enjoy the outdoors." She made a broad sweeping gesture. "You can see the area is too small to do much of anything now, and our privacy fence isn't sturdy."

"And it only covers a small area." Enthusiasm roused Karen as she thought about what the charity could do. The vision gave her motivation to learn to make wonderful apple pies. "I'm thrilled to be part of this fund-raiser, and I hope it's a success."

"Thank you so much," Nadine said, opening the door to the inside.

"You don't seem to have many children here now."

"They come and go. We're always happy when the situation changes so our families can go home. We have only the two children here now. Sad to say, when we have more kids, they at least have someone to play with."

Karen understood that, too. "Do you have one small need that I might do for you now? Anything."

"We always need personal hygiene products—soap, shampoo, deodorant, things like that."

"Then I'd like to help with that. I'll go shopping and pick up a few things for you."

"You've been a blessing," Nadine said. "I've spent a lot of prayer time focused on the needs here, and your visit has been the answer to them."

Karen was touched by her comment. She said good-bye to Nadine and thanked her for her time. Outside, she breathed in the fresh air and praised God for giving her the opportunity to serve a worthy cause. Though pleased that she could buy a few items to make life easier, Karen focused her thoughts on the plight of the children. They needed a place to play and to grow strong. They needed to see the sunlight and not be bound inside a few rooms, but with the situation, she realized that was almost impossible. She grieved for the situation.

Eric stood beside his car, his hip leaning against the side panel and his fingers tucked into his jeans. "Well?"

"This is the place. They have so many needs. I'm going to shop for some soap and shampoo—things like that—and bring them back. They have a great need here, and it's such a wonderful cause."

Eric brushed her arm as if wiping off specks of dirt, but Karen wondered if it was his way of saying he agreed.

"I thought you'd see their plight," he said. "I was touched by their need, too. That's why I volunteered."

"You're a nice man, Eric."

He drew his head back as if her comment startled him, but a silly grin made her know he'd feigned the shock. "You think so?"

Eric wasn't only nice. He was special. Karen had to believe his volunteering at the facility was an unselfish act of kindness. She'd seen his compassion and sensitivity to the predicament of displaced families. "I know so," she answered.

Before she expected, they'd arrived home, and Karen waved good-bye, realizing she'd never worked the conversation into her important question—whether or not Eric was a believer. As she headed inside the house, her grandmother's caution rose in her head. The verse from Second Corinthians flared in her thoughts. "Do not be yoked together with unbelievers. For what do righteousness and wickedness have in common? Or what fellowship can light have with darkness?"

With God's Word echoing in her head, Karen envisioned Eric's playful smile and teasing ways, his gentle kindness. *Lord, give me an opportunity to ask the right question, and if the occasion does arrive, give me courage to ask.* She knew fear held her back from knowing the truth. Ignorance is bliss. But was it? Ignorance was just plain old ignorance. She needed backbone and grit.

Where else could she find such strength, but in the Lord?

❧

Eric headed across the dewy grass to the Chapman roadside stand. He'd seen Karen heading that way and assumed she was there. When he reached the front, he was disappointed to find her grandfather seated there, too.

Walter gave Eric an unwelcome greeting, but Karen's smile made him feel better.

"What are you up to?" she asked.

"Gramma Bea wants some apples to make applesauce." He looked at one variety and then the other. "Which is best?" He aimed the question at Karen's grandfather.

"Macintosh makes the best sauce and pies," he said. "The others are eatin' apples."

"Gramma wants a peck." He lingered there, wanting to talk, but Walter put a damper on the situation.

Walter lifted the peck and set it in front of Eric. "No charge. Tell Bea it's payment for the chicken soup. If it weren't for her soup, I would've had to pay a doctor bill."

"You sure?" Eric asked.

He nodded and lowered himself into the chair.

Eric felt disappointed. He'd longed to talk privately with Karen, but that was impossible with her grandfather here. When he looked at Karen, he sensed she was disappointed, too, but he couldn't linger. He had the apples, and that's partially what he'd come for. "Thanks. Gramma will appreciate it."

"Welcome," the older man said.

Eric hoisted the peck onto his hip and turned away, but before he took two steps, Karen stopped him.

"Grandpa, I'm going to walk over with Eric for a minute."

He heard a harrumph and a grumble, but Karen joined Eric anyway.

"I wanted to talk with you," she said.

"I guessed as much." He gave her a sideways smile. "Anything in particular?"

"My Friend's Place."

Disappointment nipped at him. He'd hoped it might be about them. "What about it?"

"The children. I can't get them out of my mind."

He didn't understand, and her comment caused him to pause and face her. "I still don't understand."

"I was thinking about inviting the two—the boy and girl who were there—to visit the farm. They need a place to run and play. A place to get some sun. They've been cooped up in those rooms. It's just heartbreaking."

The peck felt heavy, and Eric shifted it to his other arm. "But I don't think that'll help. It may just cause problems. One day in the life of those kids won't make much difference."

"It's one special day in their lives."

"But you can't save the world's ills, Karen. I give you credit for trying."

She shook her head. "You're wrong. With God's help, we can do mighty things. Are you a believer, Eric? The Lord can move mountains. Do you have faith?"

Eric grinned. "Sure, but did you ever notice God, who's supposed to be all powerful, can't seem to heal our families' feud?"

Her shoulders slumped, and Eric was sorry he'd teased her. "Don't let me stop you. If you want to bring the kids to the farm, you need to make sure Nadine thinks it's okay, and then you need their mother's permission. If they both agree, it's a done deal as far as I can see."

Karen nodded, but the light had faded from her eyes. "I'm going to pick up some of those products this afternoon and drive over there. I'll ask then."

Seeing Karen's reaction to his baiting her, Eric knew he'd made a mistake. She held her faith too seriously to toy with. "I'm sorry. I was only teasing. Could I go along? I'd like to pick up a few items, too. I'm sure they could use everything we bring along."

She gave a half shrug. "It doesn't matter. If you want, I guess." She motioned toward the produce stand. "I'd better go."

"How about after lunch?"

"Sure," she said. "One o'clock?"

He agreed and watched her walk away. Eric knew he'd messed up good. In the midst of his irritation with himself, he wondered why Karen had asked. Did she really think he wasn't a Christian? The possibility startled him.

≈

Karen looked into her hand basket and eyed the items—soap, shampoo, toothbrushes, toothpaste, and deodorant. That was a start.

"What about combs and hair stuff?" Eric asked.

Karen hadn't quite gotten over Eric's comment earlier that day. She wondered if he was a Christian in name or in his heart. Today, she watched him live the faith he professed as he helped her do the shopping for My Friend's Place. She grinned at his words. "Hair stuff? Like curlers and clips?"

"And those ponytail things and the headbands. Little girls would even like those."

Eric's soft heart caught her up short again. He riled her with his teasing, then melted her to a puddle. "I'm sure they would."

"And lotion. That good-smelling stuff."

Karen followed him along the aisle, adding body lotion and hair stuff, as Eric called it. When the cashier rang up the sale, they looked at each other, seeing the cost.

"No wonder the facility likes donations," Eric said, pulling out his wallet. "Let's split half and half."

Karen agreed, but she still wanted to check out the dollar store. They always had bargains. When they exited the pharmacy, she guided him down a few stores. "They have great bargains here. Nothing more than one dollar."

"Really?" He pulled open the door, and she stepped inside.

By the time they left the shop, they had another plastic bag filled with gifts for the facility.

"Thanks for coming along," Karen said. "The company was nice, and you shared in the cost. I appreciate that."

"I'm glad," he said, opening the trunk and dropping in the purchases, then closing it. They climbed into the car and headed toward My Friend's Place, but before Eric made the turn onto Shady Road, he veered into a roadway park and stopped the car in the parking lot.

"What are we doing?" Karen asked.

"I wanted to talk, and a park seemed more pleasant than sitting in the car." He climbed out and rounded the vehicle to open her door.

He wanted to talk. Her mind filled with questions. *What about* and *why* were foremost in her mind. Karen followed him to a rustic picnic bench, and they sat on the same side, their backs against the table.

"First," he said, "I want to apologize for my curt comment earlier. I was joking, but it didn't come across that way, I guess."

"You mean the one about God being all powerful?"

He nodded and pinched his bottom lip. "I thought you knew I was a Christian. I never even considered that you didn't."

His testimony settled over her with a mixture of relief and joy. "How would I know?"

His laugh filled the air. "I'm not sure. I knew you were. I just assumed."

"You've never mentioned praying or going to church, nothing that would lead me to believe you were a believer, and my grandfather said your grandfather is a heathen."

Once the words were out, she saw them for what they were. "I'm sorry, Eric. I suppose your grandfather would be a heathen in my grandpa's eyes if he were part of the clergy."

"I think you're right," Eric said. He rested his elbows on his knees, braced his hands together, and cupped his chin on them. "I don't talk much about my faith. I came from a home where men didn't discuss their feelings openly. . .or their beliefs. Men had to be strong and stand on their own feet. Even if God could give them aid, a man was supposed to handle his own problems."

"Your father's philosophy?"

He nodded. "He was a good dad. He even went to church occasionally, but I don't know if he accepted Jesus as his personal Savior. I learned a lot of that on my own and from my grandmother."

Karen thought of the church. She hadn't seen Gramma Bea there either. "Does she go to church?"

"Most every Sunday. We go to the small Sonshine Community Church. Sun is with an O."

Sonshine Community. The name lifted Karen's spirit and made her smile. "I've never seen you at First Christian. I wondered."

"Gramma likes the simpler service. She's not into crowds too much."

Karen felt ashamed of her judgmental attitude. She'd made an assumption—a bad one. "I'm sorry, Eric. I was afraid to ask, and the longer I waited the more I assumed you weren't."

"Why were you afraid to ask?"

His question hit her bull's-eye like an arrow. How could she explain that away? Reasons came to mind—*because I like you so much I was afraid to learn you weren't a believer* or *because I'd like to spend time with you, and I'm afraid I'll get too attached.* Or the truth? *I'm falling for you.*

The silence hung above them, and she squirmed against the table back. "I—I like you a lot, and I hate to think of you missing out on heaven." That was true, but she felt so much more, yet she couldn't admit where her heart was headed.

His face reflected puzzlement, then he nodded. "Thanks.

You can stop worrying."

"I'm glad," she said. "I should have asked you long ago."

"I wish you had."

He rose, and she followed. They walked slowly across the grass saying nothing, and their feet crunched against the gravel in the parking lot. They spoke little as they finished the ride to My Friend's Place. Karen wondered what had happened. They'd talked so congenially, so naturally, until the final question. She'd been too evasive, but a woman wasn't supposed to declare her feelings for a man before she knew how he felt. That's how she'd been brought up.

Karen and Eric, now familiar and safe faces at the shelter, delivered the bags of gifts to a smiling Nadine.

"I can't tell you how wonderful this is," the woman said. "You've been so kind to us, and on top of that, you're planning a benefit for the shelter. God has blessed us more than I can tell you."

"You're welcome," Karen said. She faltered, not wanting to ruin the lovely moment. "I do have a personal question to ask."

Nadine's smile shifted to curiosity. "Yes?"

"Are the two children still here? The ones we talked about? I don't know their names."

"Yes. They're here. Dylan and Hailey." She still looked curious.

"My grandfather has a farm with lots of land, and I wondered if it's against the rules for the children to come there for a visit. I realize they can't be in town, and I'd certainly keep my eye on them."

"That's very kind, Karen. I don't think we have a policy to cover this kind of situation. We do take the families on picnics occasionally, so I don't see anything wrong with that, but you'd really have to talk to their mother, Ada."

"I understand. That's not a problem, but I hate to ask in front of the children in case she says no."

"They're on the patio, I think. I'll call Ada in to talk with you while I keep tabs on the kids."

She stepped away, and in minutes, the woman with the sad eyes appeared in front of Karen. When Karen finished her offer, Ada's eyes filled with tears.

"They'd love to go to a farm, but are you sure you want to handle two rambunctious kids? They've been cooped up here for weeks."

"I can handle them. I can't see a problem at all."

"Praise the Lord," Ada said. "I've felt so badly for them, and this is such a kind offer. When did you have in mind?"

"Tomorrow?"

"I'll have them ready."

Karen shook the woman's hand. "I'll be here after breakfast. They'll have a whole day to enjoy themselves."

❧

"That worked out better than I thought," Eric admitted, as they returned to the car. He'd loved watching Karen talk to the woman. Her excitement was as fresh as newly picked peaches, and the thought tickled him as much as peach fuzz.

"Now I have a million things to do," Karen said.

"Like what?"

"Buy some food kids like, think of activities for them—all kinds of things." She gave him a look as if to ask why he didn't realize she had all those things to do.

"I imagine they'll just enjoy the freedom, Karen. Don't make things so organized they can't just be creative kids." He slipped his arm around her shoulder and gave her a playful squeeze.

Karen laughed. "You're right."

Eric let his arm linger across her back, and his hand brushed the smooth skin on her upper arm. Holding her there seemed right, and he wished he didn't have to let go, but he did. She gave him a questioning look, and he stepped away.

They climbed into the car, and she was quiet. Eric didn't disturb her thoughts. He had thoughts of his own. . .like how much he enjoyed her company and what it might be like to date her.

"I don't have swings or slides—nothing for them to play on outside," Karen said, breaking the silence.

An idea popped into Eric's head. "No slide, but I think we can come up with a swing."

"Really?" Her face lit up like the sun. "How?"

"You just wait."

He ignored her questions, and when they pulled into the driveway, he sent her home, then hurried into the backyard, and opened his grandfather's shed. An old tractor tire leaned against the wall. A tire swing. He hadn't seen one of those in years, and he suspected those kids had never seen one. He searched the shed for rope. Disappointed, he found none. He'd have to go back into town. When he stepped outside, his pulse skipped a beat. Extended behind the shed and attached to a pole was a long stretch of rope, up and then back again. Enough for his purpose.

He looked toward the house and prayed his grandmother hadn't planned to hang out the laundry. He'd buy her another coil when he went into town. She had a clothes dryer, but she always said there was nothing like sunshine.

Eric detached the rope and tossed it over the fence, then hoisted the tire, which took more strength than he'd considered. A large oak tree stood beside the shed where Walter kept his produce, and Eric hung the loop of rope over his shoulder then rolled the tire to the tree.

"What are you doing?" Karen asked, jumping from the top porch step to the ground and darting across the lawn. She grinned when she saw his surprise. "A tire swing."

He nodded. "I bet those kids have never had one of those."

"I haven't, either," she said.

Karen seemed as anxious as a child awaiting Christmas. Together, they strung the rope and tire to the tree. When it was finished, they stood back and gazed at their handiwork.

"Can I give it a try?" Karen asked.

He grinned and helped her slide her legs into the opening. Once she was situated, he stood back and gave the tire a push. The tire spun in circles as it flew backward, while Karen's laughter filled the summer air.

When she'd had enough, Eric caught the tire and slowed it. His chest tightened as he looked into Karen's shining eyes. Her cheeks glowed with happiness, and at that moment, she was the most beautiful woman he'd ever seen.

"Help me out of this thing," she called.

Eric supported her back as she pulled one leg, then the other from the tire. He lowered her to the ground, and she stood so close he could smell the flowery scent of her shampoo. Her lips curved to a smile as she looked up at him, and it was all he could do not to kiss them.

He steadied himself, then stepped back, fighting his longing. Karen needed time to get to know him. If he acted rashly, he'd chase her away like a frightened bird.

This lovely bird he wanted to keep.

nine

Karen stood back and watched the two children run across the backyard with the freedom of a new colt. Hailey was eight and Dylan was ten, as she had guessed. On the way to the farm, Dylan wanted to know if he could milk the cows. He didn't seem too disappointed when Karen explained the farm was small and had only a garden and apple orchards.

Hailey was excited when she saw Karen's grandfather at the roadside stand as they pulled up. Karen knew better than to allow them to stand in full view on the highway, not knowing who might see them. Instead, she led them to the backyard, and once they saw the space, they galloped around, checking out the produce shed, the vegetable garden, and the tire swing.

"Can we ride on this?" Hailey asked.

"You're too small," Dylan said, obviously wanting to be the first one going for a ride.

Karen moved toward the tire. "I think she can handle it."

Dylan looked as if he wanted to protest, but he didn't. He stood back and helped his sister settle safely onto the swing. He gave a small push, and the tire swayed forward and back, but the second push sent the tire on a spiral ride. Hailey's squeals of joy rang across the grass.

"What's all the noise?"

Karen grinned, seeing Eric at the fence. "We're having fun. Jealous?"

"I sure am," he said, bracing himself on the picket bar and leaping over. "Now don't you try that," he said to Dylan.

The boy eyed the fence as if to question whether or not he

was tall enough and strong enough to make it. He apparently decided he wasn't because he turned his attention back to the swing. "My turn," he called.

Hailey gave a whine but gave up gracefully when Karen stopped the swing and let Dylan climb on. This time Eric gave a big push and the tire went spiraling into the air. The boy's delight caused them all to laugh with him.

Karen admired Eric's ability to entertain the children. He organized a flying disc game, and when Hailey got bored, Karen took her into the house to help with lunch.

"Would you like to go to the woods after we eat?" Karen asked. "We can climb trees, and then on the way back, we could pick apples."

"Off the trees?" Hailey asked, her eyes as wide as pancakes.

"Right off the trees. I love climbing in the woods," Karen said. "I sit on a limb and feel close to God."

"Do you go that high?"

Karen smiled. "Not as high as heaven, but pretty high."

"I wish I could climb to heaven." Her face twisted with her thought.

"You do? How come?"

"My real daddy's there."

Karen's voice caught on a knot in her throat. "I didn't know that."

The child nodded, and Karen could only imagine the wonderful "daddy" memories that had become shattered by the acts of Hailey's stepfather. She busied herself, keeping her tears at bay.

No matter what disappointments Karen had felt in her family life, she praised God for giving her a solid home and loving parents.

❧

"How am I going to work off this big belly?" Eric asked, pushing away from the kitchen table and patting his stomach.

The children giggled at his action.

"Karen said we're going to the woods after lunch," Hailey said.

"What's the woods?" Dylan asked, to Eric's surprise.

Eric ruffled his hair. "Trees."

"Can we climb?" the boy asked, his eyes brightening.

Karen rose and began moving the soiled dishes. "What good are trees if we can't climb?"

At the mention of the woods, everyone rose and helped Karen clear the table, and soon they headed across the meadow, carrying baskets to gather apples on the way back.

"There's the orchard," Karen said, motioning to the spread of trees in neat rows.

"I can see one," Hailey piped, jumping and pointing toward the red orbs that hung on the branches. Karen grabbed two and gave one to each.

Once they'd reached the woods, a natural hush fell over the four. Birds chittered, and brush rustled. The children's gazes darted from one spot to another, as they pointed out a chipmunk or squirrel. Eric couldn't believe the simple things he took for granted enthralled them.

"Here we are," Karen said, pointing to the sprawling oak.

"Can you climb up there?" Eric asked.

Both children nodded, but Eric prayed they were right. Karen went first, followed by Hailey and Dylan. Eric stayed below to make sure they were moving safely among the limbs, and when he was confident, he joined them.

Today Karen didn't go as high as she did alone, but it was enough to thrill the children.

"Everything looks different from up here," Hailey said. "And I could see far if the trees weren't in the way."

"That's sort of the way life is," Eric added. He gave Karen a grin, and seeing her smile, he knew she understood.

"This is like an old-fashioned world," Dylan said, "like when people were lumberjacks like Paul Bunyan."

"You know about Paul Bunyan?" Eric said. "That's great."

"I know something," Hailey announced. "It's another old-fashioned place. We learned about it in school."

"What is it?" Karen asked, her face as glowing as the sun that filtered through the tangle of leaves.

"It's called Mack-nack, and it's an island that only has horses and carriages."

Karen clapped her hands. "Good for you, Hailey. The island is Mackinac, but it's pronounced Mackinaw. . .like the city." She spelled out the two locations.

Dylan screwed up his face "Why does it have two names that sound alike but are spelled different?"

"It's very complicated. The area was named by Indian tribes," Karen said. "When the French heard what the Indians called the island, they spelled it like the French language. The letters *ac* in a word have an *aw* sound, but when the British settled in the city across from the island, they'd only heard the name and never saw it spelled, so they spelled it with the *aw*. Is that confusing?"

"Kind of," Hailey said.

"It's even confusing to grown-ups who live in Michigan," Eric added.

Karen laughed. "You aren't kidding." She ruffled Hailey's blond hair. "Did you know that we're only about an hour from Mackinaw City? That's where you get the ferry boat to the island."

"Really?" The little girl's voice was an awed whisper. "I wish I could go there."

"They have bicycles on the island, too," Eric said. "Horse and carriage, horseback, and bicycles. If you don't want to travel that way, guess what you have to do?"

Both children shrugged.

"Walk," he said.

The children giggled at his answer.

"When I first met Karen, she was sitting in this very tree." Eric recalled the day so vividly. He could almost remember their dialogue.

"This tree?" Hailey patted the bark and tilted her head.

"For sure," Eric said. He told them the story, and they laughed at the part about the shoes. "Karen likes to sing up here. . .just like one of the birds."

"Can we sing?" Hailey asked.

Karen sat quietly a minute and pinched her lower lip. "Do you know 'Jesus Loves Me'?"

They both nodded.

Karen began, with the children chiming in after her. Eric listened to their voices drifting through the limbs and wondered what a stranger wandering through the woods might think of three people singing from the branches of a tree.

It didn't matter because he knew the Lord was in heaven, smiling. So was Eric's heart.

❧

Eric sat at the dinner table, holding back his news until they'd eaten. He'd heard from the Realtor, and the sale had gone through smoothly. He owned the property and the small building. Once the renovations were complete, he'd have his market. He could no longer contain his joy, and before they'd finished, he burst out the news.

"You bought a building?" his grandmother said.

"And the property under it," Eric added, giving her a teasing wink.

"Now what in land's sake are you going to do with a building?" his grandfather asked.

"Open a health-food store. More like a whole-foods market, really, with natural products and health food. Homegrown produce." He pushed aside his grandfather's negative response. That was his way. "I'll be moving to Gaylord, naturally."

"Moving here?" His grandmother leaped from her chair

and wrapped her arms around Eric's neck. "I couldn't ask for anything better."

"You mean we'll see you more often?" Lionel's negativity weakened at the prospect. "That'll be okay."

Eric grinned, and when they quieted, his thoughts turned to Karen. Finally he could tell her his plan. No one could change his mind now. The deal was settled. He planned to see Karen right after dinner.

Later when Eric stood at the Chapman door, no one answered. Both cars were in the driveway, so he wandered into the backyard. The shed stood open, and Eric saw the baskets and dolly missing. Immediately he knew where they had gone.

The apple orchard.

He slid his baseball cap on backward and headed across the meadow. White and yellow butterflies skittered along the wildflower tops, and bees hummed in the early evening heat. Already he could smell the scent of drying grass and leaves turning crisp in the late summer sun. Hints of autumn hung on the air, a newness with each season—so much like life.

Ahead he caught sight of Walter, his arms raised above his head, and farther on, he saw Karen standing high on a ladder propped against a limb. As he neared, the sweet aroma of warm apples filled him with a sense of comfort. These fragrances were home.

God had been good to him. Despite his sins and mistakes, the Lord had blessed him with an abundant life—not wealth, perhaps, but richness of the spirit. A tingle of sadness washed over him when he recalled how Karen had thought he wasn't a Christian. He brought that on himself, he supposed. Eric hadn't been a good witness to his faith. He knew it was something he needed to change. . .something to pray about.

"Hi," Karen called, seeing him approach.

Her grandfather gave a brief nod and continued plucking apples from the branches.

"Can I help?" Eric asked.

Karen chuckled and climbed down the ladder. "How about you heading up there, and I'll keep my feet on the ground for a while."

"Happy to," he said, taking her place on top of the ladder.

Karen's grandfather paused and eyed the two of them. "If you're both going to pick, I think I'll take a break."

"You should, Grandpa. You look tired." She gave his arm a pat. "I'm tired, and I'm a little younger than you are."

"I'd say so." He lifted his gaze toward Eric. "Sure you don't mind helping out?"

"I'm happy to, sir."

Walter paused a moment, then gave his head a decisive nod. "You're a good man." He adjusted his straw hat and strutted away through the trees.

Eric gaped at him in surprise. When he turned toward Karen, her look echoed his amusement. "Now that's a change." Puzzled, Eric scratched his head.

"Praise the Lord," Karen said. "Wonders do happen." She shook a finger at Eric. "Oh ye of little faith."

He doffed his cap. "I admit it. I was wrong."

Eric picked a few apples, wondering when a good time to talk might be. Knowing his news would require explanation and some apologizing, Eric decided to wait until they loaded the dolly and started back.

The conversation was only snatches of comments and grunting sounds as each stretched for the ripe fruit. Finally, when Eric thought his back would break, Karen suggested they stop.

"I've been thinking about Hailey and Dylan," Karen said, as they loaded the baskets onto the dolly.

"What about them?"

"They had such a great time, I'd like to bring them back again."

Eric settled the final peck of apples onto the dolly. "I see nothing wrong with that, but don't get too attached. One day they'll be gone."

"So will I, soon, but that's life. Things come and go, but while they're here I can offer them some fun."

"I suppose," he said, while his mind adhered to her comment that she'd be gone soon.

Karen grasped the dolly handle then paused. "What I'd really like to do is take them to Mackinac Island. They'd love it."

"You'd be taking on a big job. Two kids, you, and a huge lake."

"Party pooper."

They grabbed the dolly handle and realized they were facing a difficult job pulling the cart along the meadow path.

"We probably overdid it on the apple picking," Karen said, "but if we left them, they'd become bird feed."

"Or worm houses."

"True," she said, a grin spreading over her face.

They unloaded a few pecks and tugged the dolly onto the path. As they walked, Eric told her his news about the property.

Karen's face moved from a smile to surprise to a frown, leaving Eric confused.

"I thought this would be wonderful for the community," he said. "I hinted about this to you in the grocery store the other day, but as I said, I didn't want to give out details until everything was settled."

"It might be fine for the community, but how will this be good for farmers? In my mind, your store will hurt them."

Her comments shocked him. "But I can sell their produce in the store. Like I said, they won't have to worry about cold or rainy weather. No spending time sitting at the roadside. They have freedom."

"Freedom to do what?"

"Well—" He stopped to give that some thought. "Freedom to do what they want to do."

"They want to grow and sell their produce."

"They can, Karen, in my store. I don't understand why you can't see that. I really thought someone like your grandfather would love this." His stomach knotted, and the afternoon pleasure darkened as quickly as the setting sun. "Why wouldn't farmers want to sell their produce in my market?"

"Pride. Farmers are proud of what they grow. They like to show off their wares and compare the size of their tomatoes to the next farmer's. You don't know much about farming, do you?"

"I thought I did."

"I think you don't."

She gave a tug on the dolly handle and quieted. He walked beside her, but he'd lost his spirit and excitement for the new market. He had other products to sell, but one of his personal joys was to help the local farmers. Could he have been wrong?

ten

Karen set the last of the vegetables onto the stand. She shifted the half-emptied baskets away from her feet and stretched her neck upward to alleviate the tension. Her conversation with Eric settled on her like a semi truck. She assumed Eric had good in mind, but all she could see were the problems for her grandfather. Why stop at a roadside stand when the same thing was available in town at Eric's market?

She heard her grandfather's footsteps crunch in the gravel, and she forced herself to look pleasant. He'd want to know what was wrong, and at this point, Karen didn't want to tell him about Eric's proposed market. He'd been feeling down as it was, and his health had become Karen's major concern.

Walter settled in his chair and eyed her handiwork. "You're setting up the stand like a pro."

She gave him a hug before joining him in a canvas chair. "Thanks. I learned it from the master."

He sent her a warming smile.

The sky above them looked clear and bright blue. The temperature had cooled, and Karen hoped for a pleasant day, despite all her concerns. As the comfortable thoughts ran through her, sprinkles fell against the stand then struck them behind the counter.

Knowing rain was impossible, Karen rose and looked to her right. She eyed Lionel Kendall adjusting his high-powered sprinkler on the edge of his property. The water sprayed across his property line, striking the side of the stand and going beyond where customers would select their produce and in the area they would park.

When her grandfather realized what was happening, he stood and gave a yell, his fist shaking in the air, but Lionel turned his back and strode into the house.

"Sit down, Grandpa," Karen said, more determined than ever to end this foolish, unchristian rift. "I'll take care of it."

Her grandfather crumpled into his chair, while Karen strode around the stand heading for the Kendalls'. But before she took a step, the water halted. She looked toward the neighbors' house, expecting to see Eric. Instead, Gramma Bea stood beside the outside spigot.

She turned and made her way across the damp grass. "I'm sorry," she said, facing Walter. "I can't answer for my husband. Sometimes he goes too far."

"We don't blame you," Karen said, feeling sorry for the sweet woman who had to deal with her husband as if he were a child. Recalling the debris fire in their backyard, she knew her grandfather behaved the same at times.

"Karen's right," Walter said. "Don't go frettin' over it. He'll get his comeuppance when he faces the Lord."

Gramma Bea smiled, probably thinking the same thing Karen was. Both men would have some tall explaining to do. The older woman eyed the bright red tomatoes and slid a quart basket toward Karen. "I'd like these and a half-dozen corn. I'll run the money back later."

"No money needed," Walter said. "Just knowin' Lionel's eatin' my produce is worth all the money in the world."

"You're a rascal yourself, Walter," she said, and waved away his words.

As Karen bagged her corn and tomatoes, Gramma Bea moved closer. "I wanted to tell you how nice I think it is that you're bringing those children over to play. Eric told me."

"I enjoy it as much as they do." Karen set the bags in front of her.

"No matter. It's wonderful. The poor children aren't to

blame for their parents' problems and sins, but they sure do suffer for them. You're doing what Jesus tells us to do—open our arms to children and people in need."

"She's takin' them on a trip," Walter said.

"A trip?" Gramma Bea asked.

Karen didn't want to be fussed over. She was doing what she thought was right. "Just up to Mackinaw City and then to the island. They were so curious about a place with no automobiles and so excited telling me what they knew about the island that I couldn't resist. We're going there tomorrow. We'll be leaving early so we have all day."

Gramma Bea frowned. "You're going to handle two children alone?"

"Just them and me. They're good kids." She wondered why Eric's grandmother seemed so concerned. "Keep us in your prayers, though. We can always use the blessings."

"Oh, I will," she said, loading the two bags into her arms. "I'll try to keep Lionel away from the sprinkler. We can both add that to our prayers."

Karen gave her a wave good-bye. Too bad Gramma Bea's good nature didn't rub off on her husband.

Then Karen's thought reversed itself. Too bad she couldn't teach her grandfather something about Christian behavior.

❧

The new building took a big bite out of Eric's time. He had to hire construction workers to do the renovations, and he'd begun contacting whole-food distributors for catalogs of products. He hoped to open the store before Thanksgiving. Though Gaylord wasn't the hugest town, many smaller towns nearby would welcome a new and unusual store to the area, he hoped. Research said he was right.

Though busy, he tried numerous times to talk with Karen, but she seemed to give him curt answers, and her geniality had turned from hot chocolate to a fudgsicle. He'd watched her entertain Ada's children, but she didn't welcome him when he dropped by, so he left, wondering what he had done to upset her.

He knew she didn't like his store idea, but he was giving that thought. She didn't give him a chance to tell her. Grudges. Feuds. He didn't understand them, and he wondered why someone like Karen, who disliked the dispute their grand-fathers had carried on so long, was acting very much the same.

As he pulled into the driveway, Eric saw the roadside stand set up to catch the Friday afternoon traffic. He admired the way Karen's grandfather seemed to understand the community. He knew the best times to be outside. Every store owner should have that kind of sympathy for his customers.

When he stepped from the car, Eric headed toward his grandparents' house then stopped. Why was he running away from Karen? If she had something to say, he wished she'd say it. He'd finally made progress with Walter Chapman, and now Karen was giving him a rough time. What happened to her Christian attitude?

Instead of going inside, he backtracked and strode toward the roadside stand. If Karen didn't want to talk with him, he could at least chat with her grandfather. "How's the roadside business today?" He focused on Walter.

"Not bad." He jingled his money box.

"That's good news," Eric said, letting his gaze drift to Karen.

"We'd have done better, except your grandfather turned the sprinklers on us." Her voice was spiked with irritation.

Eric looked at her, then his grandparents' lawn. Sure enough, the sprinkler was set at the edge of the property. "Did you turn it off?" He'd truly hoped she might have eased up by now and understood what he wanted to do with the market.

"Your grandmother did," Karen said. "She came over for some veggies."

He could picture his grandfather eating Walter's produce,

and the vision made him grin.

Karen's gaze was aimed at a car pulling alongside the road. Two people left their car and came to the stand. They seemed to be friends of Walter's, and as he chatted, Karen stood with her arms folded across her chest.

Eric took advantage of the moment and sidled beside her. He decided the direct approach would save a lot of time. No hemming and hawing today. "You're angry with me?"

"No. Not angry."

"Upset?"

"Disappointed," she said.

"About the store, I take it."

She backed away from the customers, and he followed her to the corner of the stand. "Do you see my grandfather?" she asked.

Obviously he saw him. He nodded.

"He loves talking with customers and showing off his produce. Think about that when you talk about opening a market. You're being unthinking and selfish."

Eric gaped at her. "Selfish? I thought I was offering a service to the community and to your grandfather." As he spoke, two automobiles pulled to the shoulder.

"I still think you thought wrong," Karen said as she stepped away.

"I'm sorry, Karen, I—"

She made her way behind the counter. "We'll have to talk about this later."

Later? He stepped back without saying any more. As he walked away, he sent up a prayer that God would give him a way to make things better with Karen. . .and a way to fix the problem he'd created.

❧

"Are we almost there?" Hailey piped, her nose pressed to the window.

"About halfway," Karen said, not sure, but her folks always told her that whenever they traveled when she was a child. She figured the answer worked for her. It should work for the children.

She had a difficult time concentrating. Eric filled her mind, and she felt ashamed how she'd treated him lately. Their relationship had risen above the family-feud issue with work on both their parts, but now his market plans disappointed her—not for herself, naturally, but her grandfather. Karen realized she needed to change her behavior. Even if she thought he was wrong, she shouldn't take it out on him, but she felt driven to let him know how concerned she was for the farmers in the community.

"Let's sing again," Hailey said.

The child's request jerked Karen from her thoughts. She turned toward the girl, trying to get her thoughts organized. "You like singing?"

"It was fun when we were in the tree."

"We're not in a tree now, silly," Dylan said.

Hailey's mouth turned down, and Karen knew she'd better jump in. "Not fair to your sister, Dylan. She only meant she enjoyed singing when we were in the tree."

He gave her a glance and mumbled, "Sorry."

Karen thought a moment. "Do you two know 'Jesus Loves the Little Children'?"

Hailey shook her head no.

"We know 'Jesus Loves Me,'" Dylan said.

"We sang that in the tree. How about if I teach this new one to you?"

They both turned toward her, waiting, so Karen began. She had them hum the tune with her and follow the words, and soon they were singing about all the children of the world. Her spirit lifted, and the problems that had pressed against her mind vanished with the children's uplifted voices.

Who could be moody when kids were around?

As the sign appeared for Indian River, Karen's thoughts veered to a second adventure. The Cross in the Woods. "Your mom takes you to Sunday school, doesn't she?" She recalled them knowing "Jesus Loves Me."

"When we can go," Dylan said. "We haven't been to our church since we came to My Friend's Place."

Karen's heart ached, hearing him talk about My Friend's Place and knowing what they had been through. "I'm sorry you miss your church, but I thought you might like to stop and see a church in the woods."

Hailey looked at her with disappointment. "But I want to go to the island."

"We're going there," Karen said. "This will only take a few minutes, and I have a big surprise for you."

Her eyes widened. "Surprise?"

"What kind of surprise?" Dylan asked.

Karen gave them a smile. "This church is very different. It's outside, and it has a special cross."

"Is it a wooden cross like Jesus died on?" Dylan asked.

"But bigger," Karen said, looking at Hailey through the rearview mirror.

"Really?" Hailey tilted her head, as if she thought Karen was teasing.

When they pulled into the parking lot, the children's excitement faded.

"I don't see a cross," Dylan said.

Karen shooed them across the parking lot. "You just wait."

When they reached the building, she aimed them toward the side of the gift shop and past the inside chapel toward the woods behind the building. As they descended the stair steps leading to the bottom of the hill, the children let out a whoop. In front of them was a towering cross on a dais. Surrounding its base were bleacher seats arranged in wide rows.

"Do people really go to church here?" Hailey asked, skipping down the stairs.

"Sometimes," Karen said, awed as always by the gigantic structure.

"How tall is it?" Dylan asked.

"Fifty-five feet," Karen said. "It was made from one California redwood tree."

The children skittered ahead of her, their "wows" and "ohs" greeting her as she followed them.

As the children climbed the steps to get closer, Karen sat on a front-row bench and watched. In the quiet, prayerful setting, she bowed her head, this time for the children rather than her own problems. They needed God's care far more than her relationship with Eric or the family feud.

When she could capture their attention, Karen led them to the top of the hill and back to the car. The running did them good, as well as seeing the cross. They settled back, and before they could ask again, she took the I-75 exit ramp into Mackinaw City and drove to the ferryboat dock.

The hydro-jet boat stood at the pier. Karen paid for the tickets and hurried the children on board. Before she could stop them, they darted up the stairway to the open deck at the top of the ferry. Soon the boat began to move, and they took off for the fifteen-minute ride to the island. The children giggled as the warm wind whipped their hair into tangles. The sunshine sparkled on the water, and the waves churned away from the ferry as they skimmed the water.

"The American Indians who lived here called this island *Michilimackinac*," Karen said. "Do you know why?"

Both heads indicated they didn't know.

"They thought the island looked like a great turtle, and that's what the word means."

"It does look like a turtle," Dylan said, drawing the shape with his finger.

The island drew nearer, and the children craned their necks to see the view. Their excitement bubbled into their voices. "We're almost there," Hailey said, pointing to Fort Mackinac seated on the hillside and the town nestled below it.

"What's that?" Dylan asked, pointing to the long white building gracing the hillside above the town.

"The Grand Hotel," Karen said. "Wait until you see it up close. It's a very famous place."

When the ferry drew nearer, the boat nosed into shore. "Please don't start running until the ferry comes to a stop and it's tied to the pier," Karen said.

They minded, and once the go-ahead was given, the children bounced down the stairs with Karen behind them. She took their hands as they stepped across the temporary walkway onto the long wooden pier. Benches along its edge were filled with people waiting to board, and Karen kept her gaze peeled to her two charges.

Hailey came to an abrupt stop and let out a whoop. "Look who's here," she yelled, then broke loose from Karen's hand, and darted off ahead, her feet pounding against the wooden pier.

Upset and bewildered, Karen followed behind her like a frightened mother hen, until she came up short and gaped.

"Hi. What kept you?" he asked.

eleven

Eric grinned at Karen's surprised expression. The children danced around his feet as if he were the Pied Piper, while Karen seemed speechless. Concerned about a confrontation, he focused on the kids when he spoke. "How was your trip?"

"We saw a cross made out of a redwood," Hailey said.

"You did? You must have stopped at the Cross in the Woods." Dylan tugged at his arm. "We climbed up and stood next to it. It was taller than you are."

Eric tousled the boy's hair. "Much taller, I'd say."

"I thought they'd enjoy seeing the cross." They were the first words Karen had spoken since she saw him. "So. . .why are we so honored?"

She'd continued down the pier as Eric followed. "I figured you could use some help."

"I'm sure we could have managed very well alone. . . ." She faltered a moment. "But it was nice of you to think of us."

She had been all he'd thought about the past couple of days, but he wasn't about to tell her.

They strode along the pier and arrived on Main Street. The Lake View Hotel spread out before them. Its turret and sprawling white porch with rocking chairs lined in a row added a unique charm to the white building. Bicycles wheeled past and carriages rolled along, their arrival announced by the clomping of horse hooves. Eric scanned the street, still amused by the charm of a town without motor vehicles.

"Ice cream," Dylan called, pointing toward Ryba's Ice Cream Shop.

"Let's wait," Karen suggested. "I thought you might like a carriage ride."

"How about renting bikes?" Eric asked, giving Karen a questioning look. "It's not too far. Just a little over eight miles around the island."

"Bikes," Dylan said. "I vote for bikes."

Hailey looked disappointed, and Karen shifted to her side. "We can take the carriage ride and let the boys ride bikes."

Eric hung on her answer. He had no desire to bike around the island without Karen. That would mess up his plan to give them some time to talk.

Finally Hailey shook her head. "No. I'll go on the bike ride, too."

Karen raised an eyebrow toward Eric. "Bikes it is, then."

She didn't appear totally happy, but Eric was. The children scampered after him to the bike rental shop only a short distance away, and within ten minutes, they were climbing onto bikes. "I still think you're wrong," Eric said. "A bicycle built for two would be fun."

"I don't do tandem," Karen said. "And it's only fun depending on who's sharing the bike."

Though she snipped her comment, he noticed a grin stealing on her face.

"Don't blame me if you get tired," Eric said.

"Me? Tired?" She sent him a facetious laugh.

He wondered if she remembered part of the ride was uphill.

They headed away from the center of town passing the fort above them on the hillside, the Chamber of Commerce building, the marina filled with sailboats, the Visitors' Center, and St. Anne's church. As they rounded the bend, the road began to climb. Eric flew along then realized he was alone. He skidded to a stop and looked over his shoulder. The children were pedaling with all their strength, but Karen had given up and was pushing her bike up the hill.

When she reached him, her faced glowed with perspiration and a frown that would win first prize. "You didn't remind me this was hilly."

"I figured you knew," he said.

The children seemed thrilled and pointed ahead to the limestone rocks jutting above the highway.

"What's that?" Hailey asked.

Eric looked ahead. "It's the Arch Rock."

"Let's go." Dylan jumped on his bike and pedaled away.

"It's flatter here," Eric said to Karen. "And remember, I offered a tandem bike. You said no."

"I made a mistake." Her response caused her to chuckle at herself.

They moved on together until they reached the children, who had paused below the rock formation.

"Can we climb the steps?" Dylan asked.

"Park your bikes at the roadside first," Eric said.

Karen watched the others secure their bicycles as her spirit toppled. She looked upward at the long flight of wooden stairs. "It's a hundred and fifty feet up there. Hundreds of steps. I don't think so."

Eric tousled Dylan's hair. "Sure we can. Last one up is a kumquat."

Karen's back straightened as she struggled for a response. He'd jumped right over what she had said.

Hailey giggled. "A what?"

"Just ignore them," Karen said, watching Eric and Dylan begin the climb. "We can stay down here and wait."

"It's a fruit," Eric called from twenty steps above them.

"I want to go, too," Hailey said, her lower lip thrust forward.

Karen swallowed and looked again at the long flight of stairs. She took a deep breath, lowered the bike stand, and hurried along behind Hailey.

She wanted to be furious at Eric, and part of her was, but

the other part reminded her that she needed to stop her uncharitable attitude. She'd criticized the families for the feud, and she'd carried her own misgivings with Eric too far. Forgiveness was the key. She knew the Bible well enough to know she couldn't distort what Jesus had said. If she wanted to be forgiven by the Father, she must forgive others.

Eric and Dylan had vanished, and halfway up, Karen and Hailey stopped to gasp for breath. The view was amazing, and Karen knew the sight from the top was even better. They started off again, and huffing and puffing, they reached the top.

"Look," Hailey said, gasping as she reached the summit, "we could have come here on the carriage ride."

Karen nodded. That's how she'd always viewed Arch Rock before, and that's how she would view it from now on.

Eric and Dylan had been leaning over the parapet as she and Hailey had struggled the last few steps. Karen heard their laughter follow them to the top.

"This is the last time I'm listening to you," Karen said, but she didn't mean it. During the final trek up the staircase, she'd admitted to herself that she'd been pleased that Eric had joined them.

Eric caught her hand. "Bad sport?"

"No, bad friend."

He gave her a quizzical look.

"Thanks for surprising us today. I'm glad you came along." She didn't pull her hand away but enjoyed the closeness. He smelled of sun and fresh air. The breeze on the bluff ruffled his wavy hair, and she longed to run her fingers through it.

"I'm glad I did, too. You know who put me up to this?"

He caught Karen by surprise. "No. . ." Then she remembered Gramma Bea's many questions the day before and knew the answer. "Your grandmother."

"Right." He squeezed her hand. "She wanted to make

sure you had no trouble keeping an eye on the kids around the water."

"Good for Gramma." Karen's pulse heightened feeling her hand in his bigger one.

"Let's go," Dylan called.

Karen grinned, understanding the children's eagerness to get moving, but at that moment, she didn't want to go anywhere but into Eric's arms.

The trip down the stairs was easier than going up, and once they'd reach the road again, they unlocked and climbed on the bikes and pedaled ahead. Some bikers flew past them, and some were on foot pushing the cycles up the hill. Along the way, carriages clomped past while tour guides told the tourists the island's history. An occasional horse and rider left the narrower paths and galloped along the road that circled the island.

The water rippled to their right, and distant boat sails fluttered against the blue sky. Even a freighter could be seen against the horizon, making its way through the Great Lakes toward Wisconsin or Chicago.

When they reached Point Aux Pins, Karen announced they were about halfway. The children's eagerness had faded, and she knew they were hungry. "If we go a little farther, we'll come to restrooms and a snack bar."

"Can we eat?" Dylan asked.

"We sure can."

"We'll stay there awhile, too," Eric said.

The news cheered them, and soon they parked their bikes near the snack bar, then made their way to the menu attached to the wooden building. Eric insisted on paying for their lunch. They balanced hot dogs and chips, along with a cold drink, toward the water's edge, where they found an empty picnic table.

Immediately the air was filled with squalling seagulls, landing near the table and hovering over them, waiting for a crust of bread or a lost potato chip. The children gobbled their food then took most of their hot dog buns to feed the birds.

When they were alone, Eric slid closer to Karen. He rested his elbows on his knees and tossed a pebble from one hand to the other. His attention was focused on the children, but Karen sensed he wanted to say something. She decided to make it easier for him.

"I haven't been very friendly lately," she said. "Not just today, but for the past few days. I'm sorry. I let my disappointment get the better of me."

He dropped the pebble onto the ground and shifted toward her. "Don't apologize. I guess you were right. I was so excited about my market idea, I didn't consider the ramifications."

"Shush," she said, feeling guilty for prompting an apology.

"No. Please," he said. "I'm rethinking the idea, and I'll find a solution. Everything else is a go. I've made the deal on the property and building. The work's been contracted out, and now I can give some thought to the other matter. Hopefully I'll find a way to work things out to everyone's satisfaction."

Karen's chest tightened as she watched him struggle to explain. He'd done what he thought was right for the community, and she had been viewing it from her grandfather's point of view only. Maybe her own point of view, when it came down to it. She'd never mentioned Eric's store to her grandfather. "I'm fine with it. I appreciate your trying to make things better."

"Then I'm forgiven?"

"I hope you can forgive me."

He slipped his hand over hers. "No need. Let's forget all of this and enjoy the day."

Karen agreed. When they rose, his hand brushed against hers until he captured her fingers in his. Hand in hand, they walked toward the water and joined the children at skipping rocks and chasing the seagulls.

Watching the sun inch its way lower in the sky, Eric suggested they start back, and on the way they made a detour to admire the majestic Grand Hotel with its seven-hundred-foot veranda that could be viewed with the naked eye all the way from Mackinaw City across the straits. They pedaled past the lovely old Victorian homes then rounded the bend. Main Street was ahead of them.

After returning the bikes, they stopped for the ice cream Dylan had wanted, then waited for the ferry to take them back to the lower peninsula. Karen snuggled beside Eric on the bench, her heart lighter than it had been in days. She'd finally heeded God's urging to use wisdom, understanding, and forgiveness, and following His will, she'd gained so much more than her anger had accomplished.

She'd experienced a oneness with Eric. Karen liked the feeling.

❧

Karen scurried down the stairs and into the kitchen. "I'm sorry, Grandpa. I overslept. You should've called me."

"You were tired. Yesterday with those kids wore you out."

She glanced at the wall clock. "Yes, but now we've missed church, or else we'll get there in time for the last hymn."

Her grandfather patted the table. "Have some breakfast. We can go to the little country church not too far away. They have a later service."

"Really? That makes me feel better," she said, throwing two pieces of bread into the toaster. She sent up a prayer of thanks to the Lord for her day on the island and for the food she was about to eat. By the time she'd pulled butter from the refrigerator, the toast was ready.

The previous day ran through her mind like a wonderful movie, one she wanted to see again. She enjoyed the children, and Karen especially loved spending the relaxing time with Eric.

Her feelings had grown even stronger as she watched him with the children. He'd make a good father and a good husband.

An alarm sounded in her head. Father? Husband? She tugged the reins of her imagination. She and Eric had a long way to go before allowing that kind of fantasy to spend any time in her mind.

When she finished her simple meal, she and her grandfather hurried to her car while he guided her to the church. The steeple rose about the trees, and after they came around the bend in the road, Karen was pleasantly surprised at the cozy, white church building that appeared.

She parked in the small parking lot, and they hurried into the building. A piano sounded as they came through the doorway, and they found a seat midway down the center aisle. When Karen opened the program, she read the church's name. Sonshine Community. The name struck a familiar cord. Then she remembered. Eric's church.

Karen let her gaze scan the congregation, and to her delight, she spotted Eric and Gramma Bea ahead of them. She grinned to herself, thinking perhaps the Lord had been at work again. Today eased her concern about Eric's faith. She still didn't know what was in his heart, but she felt compelled to believe he knew Jesus as she did. How could she judge his beliefs? Often her own behavior seemed as shaky as a baby's rattle.

The joyful service inspired Karen. Though a small congregation, the spirit was abundant. The songs rang in the rafters, the pastor's message filled her with God's love, and the offering plate overflowed with the congregation's gifts.

Following the last hymn, Karen held back, waiting for Eric to pass in her direction. His face brightened when he saw her. Gramma Bea gave her a smile then shook her grandfather's hand. When another farmer and his wife greeted the two grandparents, Eric took Karen's arm and guided her outside into the sunshine.

"This is a great surprise," he said.

"I woke up late," Karen admitted. "Grandpa suggested we come here. He didn't tell me the church's name, so I was pleasantly surprised when I realized where I was."

"What do you think?"

"Of the church? It's very nice. Spirit filled."

"It is," he said, tucking his hands into his pockets. "I think Gramma went to your granddad's church, but felt more at home here."

Karen nodded, understanding his grandmother's feelings.

"Walk?"

"Where?" She looked around her, seeing only the gravel parking lot.

"Flower gardens," he said, tilting his head. "They're behind the church."

"Sure, but what about—"

Eric held up one finger. "They'll chat forever. This is social hour, but so you won't worry, I'll run in and tell them." He darted off while Karen waited.

In a moment, Eric returned, carrying two doughnuts. He handed Karen one on a paper napkin. "I couldn't carry two drinks without spilling them."

She laughed. "This is fine." She eyed the cream-filled fattening doughnut and hesitated, but in a heartbeat, she pushed common sense aside and sank her teeth into the sweet cake.

Eric moved along the sidewalk, and Karen followed. Each of them bit into the treat and then brushed away the evidence with the napkin. When they rounded the corner of the building, Karen stopped. "This is a beautiful place. It's a rose garden."

"Roses, but other flowers, too. It's nice in the summer." He pointed to the dried stalks of snapdragons and irises. The remnants of gold and purple yarrow greeted them around a shrub. A garden bench sat nearby, and Eric motioned toward it. "Let's sit a minute."

Karen finished the last of her doughnut, wiped her mouth, and tucked the soiled napkin into the outside pocket of her handbag. She took Eric's suggestion and settled onto the bench.

Morning had passed, and the early afternoon sun had risen above the treetops. Karen breathed in the scent of fading flowers, foliage, and a citrus aroma she knew was Eric. He smelled tangy and sweet like lemonade and ginger.

"Yesterday seemed special," Eric said. "I'm happy we resolved a few things. I had a great time."

"So did I." She looked into his eyes, curious about so many things.

Eric shifted and lifted one leg to rest his ankle against the other knee. He adjusted his sock, and Karen sensed he was thinking.

The silence was broken by the hum of a bee among the faded garden.

"Sometimes I'm startled that you didn't know I was a Christian," Eric said.

Karen opened her mouth, but he didn't let her speak.

"I'm not blaming you. I'm blaming myself. I'm not good at witnessing. That's an area I need to grow in. . .that and my teasing."

"I love your teasing. I missed that very much when I was upset."

He grinned. "You did?"

She nodded. "Some of the misunderstanding was my fault. My grandfather seemed to think you were all nonbelievers. When I told him that I didn't know about you, he said, 'An apple doesn't fall far from the tree.' I guess I didn't question that. Grandpa was wrong."

"I've been wrong, too, Karen."

"How?"

"In questioning you and your feelings. I've never told you much about me."

Karen's pulse skipped. "You haven't, and I've been curious. I felt as if you were holding something back. You seemed to avoid talking about your faith, and then when you said you were a Christian, I didn't understand why you were so evasive."

"Mixed up, I suppose. I told you not long ago, I ended a couple of years' relationship with a woman, and I've been leery."

"Leery?" Karen asked, listening with mixed emotions.

"The breakup was my choosing. I knew Janine wasn't a strong believer, but I considered her a Christian. I was luke-warm myself when it came to attending church and studying the Bible, but I know Jesus. I know He's my Savior, and His death and resurrection gives me eternal life."

Karen warmed inside at his words.

"What I thought was that Janine also held my values, but the closer I got to giving her a ring, the more I realized we were heading in two directions."

Karen listened as he told her the revelations he'd come to as he saw their lives heading in different directions.

"I love the country," Eric said. "The birds, the trees, the quiet are all gifts to me. My grandparents' farmhouse is a palace, but not to Janine."

Karen's heart filled with joy as she realized that she and Eric shared so many things. They both loved their families, despite all the problems. They enjoyed the country and didn't need a mansion to be at home. Simple and cozy was better than elegant and sophisticated any day.

"We're of like minds," Karen said. "I agree."

"I know you do, and that's what makes me think that the Lord has plans for—"

"Ready?"

Her grandfather's voice stopped Eric in midsentence. She waved to him and rose. Eric stood, too, with a look of disappointment. Karen longed to ask him to finish the sentence, but their grandparents had made their way into the garden, and they didn't have the privacy or the time to finish the conversation.

Eric stepped forward first, with Karen right behind him. Her mind ran over and over his sentence and clung to his last words—the Lord has plans for. . .

Plans? Karen longed to know, because she'd begun to have plans of her own.

twelve

Karen hurried to answer the knock. She opened the door, and two strangers, a man and woman, smiled from the other side of the screen door.

"I hope we're not too early," the man said. "Are you the home owner?"

A frown tugged at Karen's face, and she looked for some kind of sales gimmick or a catalog of fund-raiser candy. "No, I'm not. This is my grandfather's house."

The man looked at the woman then returned another genial smile. "Could we speak to him, then?"

Her grandfather hadn't felt well last night, and Karen had let him sleep in. She was about to open her mouth when a noise sounded behind her. She turned, and he appeared in the living room.

"Grandpa, someone wants to talk with you."

He gave her a blank gaze and ambled to the door.

Curious, Karen stepped back and listened.

"Hi," the man said. "We wondered if it's too early to come in and look around your place."

Walter gave Karen a wide-eyed stare before he turned to the stranger. "Yes. It is. Why are you—"

"Sorry," the man said, motioning for his wife to leave the porch. "We'll check back later."

Karen and her grandfather watched the couple head back to their car, their voices tangled in the morning sounds.

"What was that all about?" Karen asked.

"How should I know?" He closed the door. "Maybe they like farmhouses."

While Karen prepared her grandfather's breakfast, her mind jumped between concern about his health and the strangers who appeared on their doorstep.

"Feeling better?" she asked.

"Now don't you worry about me," he said. "I'm just getting old."

Karen couldn't help but worry, but she decided not to let him know. Before she returned to the city, her grandfather would have a doctor's appointment for a checkup. No arguments. She set his breakfast on the table, but before she could sit, she heard another knock at the door.

Carrying her mug, Karen went to the living room. When she opened the door, another stranger faced her. "I'd like to look at the house, if it's convenient."

Karen's mind twisted with confusion. "No. It's not convenient. Sorry. I really don't underst—"

The man looked at her uneasily. "I thought this house was for sale."

"This house?" She laughed. "No. You've made a mistake."

"But I thought. . ." The man made an empty gesture. "Never mind." He turned on his heel and marched away.

Karen watched him go. Something was up. She grabbed the morning newspaper from the porch and flipped it open to the want ads. Someone had made a mistake. Maybe mixed up some house numbers. She carried the paper into the kitchen and plopped into the chair.

"Company?" Walter asked.

"No. Wrong house," she said, not wanting to upset him. She scanned the ads, then let her gaze move slower over the house-for-sale listing. Nothing. She folded the paper.

When another knock sounded, Karen threw the paper on the floor and marched through the living room to the foyer. She flung open the door and faltered when she saw Eric. A puzzled expression covered his face.

"Whoa!" Eric said. "I'm on your side. You look like you're ready to wring someone's neck."

She shook her head. "It's been a weird morning."

Eric's face shifted to concern. "It has? What's going on? Please don't tell me the arguing has gotten so bad between our grandfathers that Walter's going to move."

"Move?" Karen studied his face. His look seemed sincere. "You're not kidding?"

"No." His arm swung backward toward the roadside stand. "I noticed one of those store-bought signs in front. FOR SALE BY OWNER. Is your grandfather really selling the place?"

"No." Air raced from Karen's lungs like a pin-pricked balloon. "So that's it. It must be your grandfather's handiwork." She beckoned him inside and related the visitors they'd had inquiring about the house.

Eric's expression looked as exasperated as Karen felt.

"I'll bring it in." He turned, headed through the door, and jumped from the porch to the ground. In a moment he returned, carrying the sign. "Enough is enough." He handed her the cardboard poster. "I have to talk with my grandfather."

"Wait," Karen said. "Talk does no good. He needs a reason to change."

Eric shifted from foot to foot, looking pensive. "Reason? You've got me." He ran his fingers across his hair. "I've talked to him. Gramma's talked. We've appealed to what Christian upbringing he has. Nothing works."

Karen's mind stretched to a possibility. "Does he know you and I have become friends?"

Eric shrugged. "He knows I talk with you, but—"

"What would happen if he thought. . . ? What if he thought we were getting serious about each other and—"

Eric's face brightened. "And he thinks we might bring the family together by getting married."

"Right." Her words and their meaning struck her. Why

had she proposed such a thing?

"It might work." Then his expression dimmed. "Maybe not, but it's worth trying."

Karen began to think nothing would work, and she was about to say so when Eric laughed.

"Funny you made that suggestion." He rubbed his chin and gave her a playful smile. "I'd come over today to see if you'd like to go to dinner. Maybe a movie."

"Why?"

He took two steps backward. "Why? You're kidding?"

Karen wished she'd phrased that more carefully. "I mean we've spent a lot of time together, but we've never had a real. . .date."

"I know. That's why I'm asking you out to dinner. I thought it was time."

His expression made her laugh. "I have a pie-making lesson with your grandmother this afternoon, so dinner tonight would be nice."

"Great. We can set a time later." He took a step toward the doorway. "What should I do with this?"

"Set it on the porch. I'll get rid of it. Thanks."

He did as she asked, then darted down the steps. When he turned toward home, he tucked his hands into his pockets and whistled.

She watched him until he and his whistle had vanished.

❧

Eric closed the passenger door, gave a tap to the window, and rounded the car to climb into the driver's seat. "Ready for this piece of information?"

Karen pivoted her head to face him, a frown settling on her brow. "Something wrong?"

"When my grandfather was in town today, he had two people ask him what he wanted for his truck."

"Is he selling it?"

Eric grinned. "No, but the sign hooked on the tailgate said

FOR SALE BY OWNER. He got a taste of his own medicine."

"I can't believe Grandpa did that. I avoided telling him about the sign. How did he know?"

"His hearing isn't as bad as he makes out," Eric said, guiding the car along the state road, amazed at what codgers both men were. "Did you get rid of the sign? I left it on the front porch."

"No. I forgot." She covered her face with both hands. "They both need a good whipping," she said behind her fingers.

Eric laughed, and so did she.

Karen became silent and looked out the window.

Eric watched the trees flash by on both sides until buildings began appearing, scattered along the roadside.

"Where are we going for dinner?" Karen asked.

"The Sugar Bowl. I hope that's okay."

Karen nodded. "I've never been there."

"The place sounds like a dessert spot, but it's not. The menu has all kinds of choices. Everything from whitefish to ribs to Greek food."

"Greek food?"

He nodded. They sank into silence again, and when they reached Main Street, he turned and found a parking place on the street. As they approached the restaurant, Eric gestured to the building. "It looks like an alpine chalet with its half-timbered walls and cedar shakes." His hand touched hers, and he wove his fingers with hers. She didn't resist, and he certainly didn't either.

"Look at the colorful glass bricks," she said, "and the stained glass. It's a beautiful place."

"Wait until we get inside," he said.

The hostess seated them in the Open Hearth room, where a chef was preparing meals beside the diners. A puff of flame shot upward on the far side of the room, and voices hollered, *"Opa!"*

Karen gave him a quizzical look. "What was that?"

"Greek food. Remember? It's *saganaki,"* he said. "Flamed cheese."

Once seated Karen eyed the unique menu, and after they'd placed their orders, she sipped her iced tea and looked around at the stained-glass window frames and cherry paneling. "This is nice."

"The food is great, too." Eric slid his hand across the tabletop and rested it on hers. "I'm glad you agreed to come. I let my grandparents know we had a date. You should have seen Granddad's face, but he didn't say a word."

She smiled. "Did he get frazzled?"

"Probably after I left."

Their food arrived, and they enjoyed the meal. The conversation was centered around Eric's business matters, and Karen's attempts at pie baking for the Arts and Apple Fest.

"I'll be a real pastry chef when Gramma Bea gets finished with me," she said. "Sometimes I wish that was the only problem I had."

"Something wrong?" He laid his fork on his plate and leaned forward on his elbows, concerned about the stressed look that appeared on her face.

"Nothing serious. You know my vacation is running out. I took extra time for Grandpa, but I'm expected back at work."

His spirit sank. He knew she would leave eventually, but he'd tried to push it out of his mind. "You like your work?"

She tilted her head back and forth. "Yes and no. I realize it's important. Being a child advocate is rewarding and challenging, but it's not the personal connection I like to have with people. I love seeing progress made, changes happening, smiles on people's faces. Even when we try to do what's best for the children, I see too many tears and so much sadness."

"I'm sure it's difficult." He didn't know what else to say to make her feel better. He watched her hand pressed against the tabletop, and he lowered his arm and wrapped his fingers around hers. "You have great credentials. Maybe you need to look for something else, a position that will use your talents, but in a more positive way."

She nodded. "I've just let things ride. The easy way out. . .but not always the best way. I suppose I should look around. Something's bound to be out there that will make me happier than what I'm doing."

He agreed.

The waitress appeared and took their plates, then offered the dessert menu. "We aren't called the Sugar Bowl for nothing," she said, her smile as broad as her frame.

Eric scanned the many options. "What's the specialty here?"

She grinned. "Warm homemade raspberry pie. Everyone loves it, and it's in season."

Karen licked her lips. "Sounds yummy."

"We'll take two orders, and make that à la mode."

"You got it," she said, gathering the menus and moving off.

Karen tilted her head, her eyes brighter than before. "So what's up with your property? Where is it, by the way?"

"It's down the street a ways. Too dark to look at now, but we can come back in the daylight. They're making progress. I hope to open before Thanksgiving."

"That's fast. I'd love to see it."

Eric feared he might bore her, but his excitement motivated him to continue and detail all the changes he'd done to the inside of the building and all the ideas he had for the future. "I have a set of blueprints in the car. It makes great reading on a date."

Karen sputtered a mouthful of iced tea. "Sounds romantic. I'll have to see them."

He loved to hear her laugh, and her reference to romance captured his imagination. What if Karen lived in Gaylord? What if a real relationship progressed? What if. . . ?

So many possibilities. So many windows the Lord was opening for them both.

thirteen

The rain seemed unending. Michigan had always been known for its unexpected change in weather, but the rain clouds had become a daily event. Thunder, lightning, and drizzle. Karen watched her grandfather pace across the living room. He'd pause to gaze into the sky then resume his journey back and forth on the carpet. She figured if the storms lasted much longer, he'd wear out the rug.

"All those vegetables are going to waste," Walter said as he paraded to and fro. "It's a pity. The apples will rot, too, unless I get them into a cool, dry place."

"When the rain stops, we'll think of something," Karen said.

Her grandfather sank into his recliner and snapped on the television. His finger hit the remote, flashing from station to station.

"What are you doing?" Karen asked.

"Looking for a weather report."

The scenes blinked past, and Karen wondered if he would miss the station in his impatience.

A rap on the door caught her by surprise. Who'd be out in this weather? She rose and strode across the room. Through the small window, she saw Eric drenched to the bone. Karen flung open the door. "What are you doing outside in this?"

"Visiting you," he said, stopping on the door rug to slip off his shoes and shake the rain from his hair.

"You must be part duck."

"I'm bored," he said, lifting his hand to acknowledge her grandfather.

"Come inside," Walter said. "But you won't find much to lift your spirits here."

Eric gave Karen a curious look.

"He's depressed because of the produce that's spoiling in the shed."

"And the rest will be drowned by the rain. I've been thinkin' maybe we should consider building an ark."

Eric chuckled at Walter's sense of humor. "Couldn't hurt." He stood near the door and leaned against the jamb. "Sorry about the vegetables. I know this is tough."

"A roadside stand is only as good as the weather. Not much else to do."

Eric's face brightened, and he moved closer. "I don't think I've told you about my new business venture. It could help farmers in situations like this."

Walter's attention perked up. "Sit. Sit. Tell me about it."

Karen cleared her throat loud enough for Eric to hear, but he seemed too bent on talking about his new store, and he missed her hint.

Eric stayed where he was. "I'm all wet, Mr. Chapman."

"Phooey! Wet dries in time. Have a seat."

Walter motioned Eric toward the sofa, but he selected a chair and sat on the edge.

"So what's this about a business venture?" Walter asked.

Eric glanced at Karen, and she did all she could to let him know, in her opinion, he was stepping on sensitive ground. Whether he understood or not, Karen never knew, but whichever, it didn't stop him. Eric began to detail his business dream. To her surprise, her grandfather leaned closer, as if interested in what Eric had to say.

"That would move the produce, at least," Walter said. "I hate to see it go to waste. Rain couldn't close a store."

Karen felt her eyebrows hit her hairline. Her grandfather's attitude startled her. She had been positive he'd be upset. Hearing him made her realize she'd been upset over nothing. She owed Eric a huge apology.

Walter scratched his head. "If I could think of somewhere to send all that food, I would."

Eric sat a moment in thought then snapped his fingers. "Why not the women's shelter? I'm sure they would love to have the fresh produce. It would help their budget."

"And rather than be garbage, it'll serve a purpose," Walter said. "Great idea."

"I'll call Nadine Smith—she's the director—just to make sure," Eric said.

Karen pointed to the telephone then listened to one side of the conversation, but already she knew that Nadine was thrilled. So was her grandfather.

When Eric hung up the phone, Karen grinned. "You don't have to tell me. I know you've made her day."

"That and more," he said. "And it's not me. It's your grandfather." He turned to Walter. "She's really happy about this and wants me to thank you."

Walter brushed off his comments, but Karen knew he was pleased to have been able to do something nice for My Friend's Place. Her grandfather loved the children around the farm. She was sure it helped distract him from missing her grandmother.

Karen found an umbrella in the closet, and she and Eric nestled close together and made a dash for the produce shed.

❧

Eric enjoyed having Karen by his side as they skipped over the puddles. He slid his arm around her back to keep them together under the umbrella, and Eric loved the feeling. Water splashed around their feet, and they were laughing as they hurried into the shed.

Karen shook the water from the umbrella then pulled the door partially closed. Eric pulled a cord that hung from the ceiling, and a small overhead bulb offered them dim light so they could work.

"I'll pull the car closer once we have the stuff packed up," Eric said, searching along the back for a box. He found a couple stacked in the corner. "Maybe the rain will pass and your grandfather will have one good day to open the stand. We should probably leave the freshest vegetables in the shed."

Karen agreed and began filling the boxes. "This was a good idea," she said. "Grandpa feels better knowing the food's not going to waste." She paused a moment, then stopped, and turned to him. "I owe you a big apology. Grandpa didn't mind your idea at all. After I acted like a jerk about it, I realized I was totally wrong."

Eric caught her hand and drew her close to him. "You weren't totally wrong, and you aren't a jerk at all. I admire you, Karen, for having such strong feelings for your grandfather. You were defending his right to his business while I hadn't given it any thought. That's noble of you."

She made a face, as if she thought he was making too much of it. "It's not noble. It's just love. I adore him and didn't want him to get hurt."

His pulse kicked into gear as he lifted his hand and brushed her cheek. "Then I admire you all the more. Love is much more important."

He felt a shudder run through her.

"Cold?"

"No. Just amazed."

He let her comment drop because he had more to say. "I want you to know I still plan to remedy the problem of the store interfering with the outside stands. Something will come to me."

She nodded and tilted her chin upward as if searching his eyes for something deeper.

Her eyes sent his heart on a whirl, an amazing sensation of spinning out of control. He captured her chin in his fingers and brushed one along her lower lip. The feeling was warm and tender. His control skidded to the edge of wisdom and dropped over the edge as he lowered his mouth to hers.

His pulse skipped when she accepted the kiss, her own hand rising to rest against his hairline. Breathless, he eased back. They said nothing but stood face-to-face as he listened to the rhythm of the rain tapping on the roof and echoing the beating of his heart.

ঌ

Uneasy, Karen sat beside Eric, pondering his kiss. She'd not pulled away but leaned into it. She felt uncertain as to its meaning but that was no surprise. She had a difficult time figuring out her own feelings.

The tender kiss had caught her off guard, but now the memory lingered in her thoughts and sent her pulse scurrying through her. Eric had mentioned his past relationship, and concern niggled her. Could his interest only be a rebound reaction? She sidled a look at his sculpted profile, his firm jaw, and the hint of a dimple beside his smile lines. She'd never noticed them until recently.

"You're quiet," Eric said, glancing her way. He shifted his hand from the wheel and brushed it against her fingers folded in her lap. "Thinking?"

She nodded.

"I hope they're good thoughts."

She realized he'd become apprehensive, probably about the kiss. Karen longed to string him along, but she didn't have the heart. "This wasn't the first time you kissed me, you know."

He glanced at her again, this time surprise on his face. "I hope you aren't angry with me."

"How could I be? I didn't fight you off."

Eric grinned. "No, you didn't." His grin turned to a chuckle. "I remember the first time we kissed. I was seven or eight, and you were a year younger. Where did I get my nerve?"

"Nerve? Where did you get the idea?" She hadn't thought

of that incident until recently. "I think you watched too much late-night TV."

"I probably saw my mom and dad kiss. They were very romantic. Properly so."

Karen chuckled. "It's nice when married couples are still in love."

"Do you remember where I kissed you?"

She nodded. "In the cornrows."

"Life was easier then, wasn't it?"

"Much easier." Karen's thoughts slid back to those days. If the grandfathers were disagreeing, she'd never noticed. "Do you remember the feud back then?"

"No, I was too busy chasing the pretty neighbor girl."

"We have to find out what caused it, Eric. I really think God brought us together to solve the problem." She shifted in the seat and adjusted her seat belt so she could face him. "Do you know what I mean?"

He paused a moment before answering. "I'd hoped the Lord brought us together for something more special than smoothing out their problems."

Special? Her heart rose to her throat and choked away her words.

"Not that I don't think we should do something, but I really like you Karen, feud or no feud."

"I like you, too," she said and wanted to say "very much," but she reined in the words. "Still, I'd feel better if we could improve the situation. I think the key is your grandmother."

"Gramma Bea? She can be a hard nut to crack. I've tried."

"We'll see," Karen said, her mind spinning with ideas. If the Lord was on her side, she knew she'd find the answer, once and for all.

When Karen focused outside, she was surprised to see My Friend's Place up ahead. Eric parked, then ran inside for a dolly. As they loaded the boxes, Nadine greeted them with open arms.

"Bless you," she said as they brought the produce inside. "God answers prayers." She shook her head as if awed by the bounty they'd delivered.

"I'm glad you can use the food," Karen said. "My grandfather didn't want to see it spoil, so your need made him feel purposeful."

"We do have need," Nadine said, joining them in unloading the boxes. "We're partially funded by the state, but most of our finances are gifts from people who care. People like you."

"Too bad you can't publicize the facility more," Eric said. "I didn't know you existed until I volunteered through the church to paint."

"That's one of our problems. I'm so busy being housemother and administrator that I don't have time to promote the facility or do fund-raising. I got word a few days ago that one of the groups that supports us is giving us a generous gift to finance a new position here. The board has already approved it, and I'm going to be looking for someone to do those jobs— letting people know we're here and promoting ways to add to our funds."

"That's great," Karen said. "That's the key to a service-oriented program like yours. I'll keep your need in my prayers."

"Thank you," Nadine said. She stood back and shook her head. "This food is amazing. Our families will be thrilled. She buried her nose in the basket of tomatoes. "Nothing smells more wonderful than sun-ripened vegetables and fruit."

"I'm sure my grandfather will be happy to send over some extra things now and then. The season is coming to an end, but until it does, you can count on us."

"These are the gifts that keep us going." She clasped her hands against her chest. "On top of that, we'll benefit from the Arts and Apple Fest pie booth. That's another gift."

"We're excited about helping," Karen said.

"Is there anything we can do here for the booth? Would some flyers help, telling people about our services?"

"Excellent," Eric said. "Every person who knows about My Friend's Place will share the information with people who need to know you're here."

"I'll see you get a stack."

"Thanks," Karen said, but her thoughts had already drifted to other matters. "How are Hailey and Dylan? The rain has kept me from coming back to take them to the farm."

Nadine's face brightened. "I'm so pleased you mentioned them." She held up one finger. "I have something for you."

Questions buzzed in Karen's thoughts, and she gave Eric a puzzled look, but he only shrugged. Within a moment, Nadine reappeared, carrying an envelope.

"This is from the kids," she said, handing it to Karen. "They've gone back home. Naturally they were thrilled, but Hailey and Dylan both said they'd miss you."

A knot caught in Karen's throat. She looked at the envelope. "What happened that they could go home?"

Sadness filled Nadine's eyes. "We were able to help Ada get a restraining order against her husband, and we had enough photographs of her condition when she arrived that the police can prosecute." She shook her head. "I get too emotional over these things. I'm happy for them leaving, but they've been through so much. Life will be harder without his income, but easier on their self-worth and safety. Ada's praying he'll get some help."

"I agree," Karen said, fingering the envelope.

Nadine gave her a nod. "Open it if you'd like."

Piqued by the sealed envelope, Karen peeled back the flap. Inside, she found two drawings, one from each of the children. Her eyes welled with tears as she gazed at them. Words wouldn't come, and she handed Eric the sketches, then brushed the tears from her eyes.

Eric gazed at the pictures, then showed them to Nadine.

"Karen took the kids to see the Cross in the Woods, and this one is us bicycling on Mackinac Island."

Karen shifted her gaze to the drawings in Nadine's hand. Hailey had drawn a picture of the majestic cross with two stick figure children standing below it. In the sky a bright sun sent rays in a large circle, but the longest rays touched the cross and the children beneath. Her childish printing read, "I love you. Don't forget us."

Forget them? How could she? She swallowed back the sob that ached in her throat. Dylan's picture showed more talent. Four bicyclists standing beneath the huge Arch Rock. A long staircase worked its way to the top, and in his simple cursive writing, he'd also left a message. "Thank you for the fun times at the farm and on the island." His spelling was perfect, and Karen read the words again as they blurred in her eyes.

"So nice," Nadine said, handing back the drawings. "You've touched two children with your love and compassion. Ada felt the same. She told me to let you know how grateful she was for your kindness." Nadine offered her hand. "I'm grateful, too."

Karen and Eric accepted her handshake, then made their way outside.

As they pulled away, Eric gave her a thoughtful look. "How's that job sound that Nadine talked about? It sounds like something you could do."

"Me?" Karen's heart skipped. "I hadn't given it any thought."

Could this be the Lord's answer to her prayers? Karen leaned against the car seat and let the question wash over her.

fourteen

Karen stood by the doorway, waiting for Eric. He'd invited her to see his property, and she had agreed. She knew he was struggling to make things right, and she admired him for that. Even though her grandfather had agreed his store was a good idea, Karen's concern had put questions in Eric's mind. He was a man of his word. Karen had learned that.

Her own thoughts snagged around questions about her work. Eric had raised a good point. She didn't have to go back to the agency in the city. The Lord opened doors and windows, and Karen knew she only had to trust in Him to guide her.

The new position at My Friend's Place banged in her thoughts. She needed to weigh the pros and the cons. Would working in Gaylord be a wise career move? Where could she go in that position? Where did she want to go? Her thoughts churned into a thick buttery mass of confusion. The possibilities lay as a lump in her mind.

Then came Eric. What was going on between them? Were her feelings premature? Had the Lord guided her to something special and lasting with Eric? The family's squabble rose in her thoughts. Maybe a serious relationship between them would make a difference between the grandfathers. As soon as the thought left her, she realized that the Lord didn't bring two people together to fall in love for that purpose. Love was a precious gift requiring commitment and devotion. Was that where her heart was leading her? Eric's image rose in her mind. No, he wasn't an Adonis, but that wasn't what she wanted. He was handsome enough, and best of all, he was filled with all the good gifts the Lord handed out.

Eric, despite all her earlier fears, was a true Christian.

Karen heard a noise and looked toward the driveway. Eric had pulled up and stepped out of his car. Before he could reach the door, she moved to the porch and met him halfway.

"You're not that eager to see my empty, half-finished building are you?"

She shook her head. "No, but I have a mind full of butter that needs making into little neat pats."

He wrinkled his nose and squinted at her as if she'd lost her head. "Huh?"

"I'll explain," she said.

He accepted that, and once in the car, she expounded on her thoughts. Karen needed pros and cons before she would even consider applying for the job in town. They tossed out ideas. Pros: She would live near her grandfather; she would have the kind of contact with people that she enjoyed; she would see positive things happening in her work; and she would feel less stress.

"That's a good start," Eric said. "How about the cons?"

"First one is much less money. I'm sure the salary couldn't touch what I'm making now. . .although that's not a fortune."

"How important is the money?" Eric asked.

She shrugged, not certain how to answer the question. "I suppose it depends where I live. In the city, things cost more. If I'm here, my costs are less."

"Then that's not a problem."

His comment took her by surprise.

"Next," Eric said and waited.

"Next?" She thought a moment. "I'd have to give up my apartment."

"And?"

She chuckled. "I wouldn't need it if I were living here."

"You could live with your grandfather until you decided you needed more independence."

"He'd be thrilled. He really misses my grandmother." The words caught in her throat.

"I'm sure he does," Eric said. "I know he's happy you're there, and I think you're relieved to be there."

She nodded. Eric was right again.

"Another con?" he asked.

"Benefits? Would I have insurance coverage? That's important."

"It is," Eric said. "You'll have to find that out when you apply. . .*if* you apply."

He turned the car into a concrete parking lot. "This is it."

The building was larger than Karen expected. She peered at the trucks and construction equipment, knowing the men were at work. She felt honored to be one of the first to see what he was doing with the building.

Eric came around to open her door, and she paused before leaving the car. "You've given me a lot to think about. I'll never know unless I apply," Karen said. She stepped to the ground, and Eric closed the car door.

"Good thinking," Eric said, brushing his fingers across her cheek.

She smiled, and he captured her hand in his then led her across the parking lot. As they walked, Karen reviewed their conversation. She'd found many more pros than cons in applying for the new position. She needed to pray about her decision and let the Lord be her guide.

Admiring Eric's profile as they walked, she sensed the Lord was leading her in his direction as well. Still, what was Eric thinking? Karen knew she could be a summer fling and nothing more. Could she trust Eric's romantic actions?

The sun slid behind a cloud, and a chill rustled through her. Faith. She needed to put it all in the Lord's hands.

❧

Eric settled onto the back porch, waiting for Karen to bring out some iced tea. Her grandfather had fallen asleep in his recliner, and they didn't want to disturb him. Eric had enjoyed the afternoon, showing Karen the building and his plans. She seemed impressed. The renovations had gone smoothly, and he anticipated the November opening as he had hoped.

"Here you go," Karen said, coming through the doorway with a tray. She carried two tumblers of tea and a plate of cookies.

"Home baked?" he asked, sending her a playful grin.

"Homemade," she said, lifting her nose in the air as if he'd hurt her feelings.

Eric took a bite of the chewing confection. "They're chocolate chip."

"I thought those were your favorite."

"They are. You remembered."

She smiled, then her expression changed, and she rose from beside him. "I have an idea." She hurried from the room.

Eric waited, wondering what thought had come to mind so quickly to motivate her to hurry from the room.

He had the answer in a moment. Karen returned carrying photograph albums. She settled back onto the wicker love seat. After laying the others on the floor, she opened one of the books and flipped through the pages.

"These are the photos I showed Grandpa when he got so moody." She tapped on a couple of pictures. "What do you think?"

He leaned down to look at the faded black-and-white photos. "Interesting."

"I thought so."

He turned the page.

"This is my grandmother," Karen said, pointing to the picture.

Eric chuckled. "Guess who's standing beside her."

Karen pushed her face closer to the photograph. "I have no idea."

"My grandfather."

Her head tilted upward like a shot. "*Your* grandfather. Lionel Kendall?"

"Uh-huh. I didn't know they'd been neighbors that long."

"Me, neither," Karen said, taking a bite of cookie.

Eric brushed cookie crumbs from the page, and curious, he flipped to another. He scanned the pictures and found one more that included his grandfather. "They must have been friends at one time." He gazed at Karen. "Doesn't it look that way?"

She nodded, her eyes wide and dazed. "I wish I could ask my grandfather about this." She shook her head. "I know he'd go into a tizzy and probably throw these away."

"Hide them."

She chuckled. "He has a nose like a bloodhound. He seems to see and hear everything."

"And smell everything," Eric said, gesturing to the trash cans along the fence as they both laughed. He looked at her sweet, smiling face and drew her against his shoulder. "I love seeing you in a cheerful mood."

"I am. I'm really feeling good and settled. I made up my mind about the job. I have an appointment tomorrow."

"Really?" He sat up straighter.

"Really." Karen shifted and felt her stomach growl. "I'm starving. Are you?"

He nodded, realizing he hadn't eaten in hours except for the cookies.

"How about staying for dinner? We can pick some corn. Think how fresh that will be."

"Sounds great." Picking corn. God couldn't have guided the occasion any better. He jumped up and helped her rise. He didn't let go of her hand as they headed outside, enjoying the closeness and the feeling of her smaller hand in his.

On the way to the corn, they grabbed a basket, and Karen dropped in a few tomatoes on the way. When they reached the field, she ran ahead, and Eric followed. . .just like years earlier when they were children. His heart galloped. When she stopped to pick a ripe ear with deep golden silk, he took the basket from her hand and set it on the dark earth.

She paused then turned to face him. He watched her expression shift from bewilderment to understanding.

"I can't let the opportunity pass," Eric said.

Her gaze locked with his as he drew her into his arms. She tilted her face upward, and he lowered his mouth, touching hers in a breathless wash of memory and delight. Eric eased back.

A tender smile curved Karen's soft lips. "Like a step back in time."

"I couldn't resist."

"I'm glad you didn't," she said.

For a moment they stood so close he could feel the warmth of her body next to his. The scent of fertile earth and plant life filled the air. His own life blossomed like new buds on the branches. He prayed that life had only begun for him and Karen, but he knew better than to rush things. She was a determined woman who had her mind set on how things should be. He wanted to make sure he was part of what she wanted.

❧

Karen pulled into the My Friend's Place parking lot. Nadine had been excited to hear from her and encouraged her to apply. Although the woman didn't have total control over the hiring, Karen hoped Nadine's recommendation would hold some weight. She sensed the woman liked her.

Snapping her thoughts closed, Karen asked God's forgiveness. She'd vowed she would put the ultimate choice in God's hands—she'd get the job or not, but she knew that the Lord knew the future and knew what was best for her. She had to let go of the decision and give God lordship over her life.

She strode across the parking lot, her mind full of purpose. Nadine opened the door as if waiting for her, and she followed the petite woman into her small office.

"Have a seat, please," Nadine said.

Karen sank into the chair and crossed her legs. "I'll be honest. I've tossed the pros and cons back and forth, trying to decide if I should apply. I've wanted to leave my present position, and this one seemed to jump out and grab me. I'm asking the Lord to lead me."

"That's the only way," Nadine said. "Funny that you mention feeling grasped by the opportunity. When I mentioned the position, I had a warmth in my heart, sensing the Lord telling me something. I wondered if it was you He was leading to answer our need." She chuckled. "You've answered it so many times already—unknowingly."

Karen could only nod, awed at the way God worked in her life. "The Lord sort of sneaks up on me and turns me around sometimes."

"Exactly." She flipped open a file and handed Karen a document. "Here's how the board envisions the new position. Take a few moments to read it. You gave me your credentials over the telephone, but I'll need them in writing for the committee."

"Certainly," Karen said, accepting the papers from Nadine, then handed her the manila envelope she'd brought with her. "Here's my résumé. This should cover everything, but if you need anything else, please let me know."

"Great." She pulled out the resume and scanned it. "I'm sure this will be fine. It's very impressive."

Karen lifted her eyes from the job description and gave her a smile. "Thanks." She returned her gaze to the papers and read. She liked what she saw and sensed the job was perfect for her. Though she'd worked as a child advocate, she had taken classes in college in management and public relations. Karen felt confident she had people skills and could handle rejection. Rejection? Most kinds, she added. Eric's rejection would be something she didn't want to experience.

Fund-raising appealed to her. Talking with people, getting

excited about what My Friend's Place had to offer people in need and finding creative ways to solicit funding all seemed to intrigue her. Even the fund-raiser coming up at the Arts and Apple Fest would let people know about the facility. The two jobs worked hand in hand.

"This looks good," Karen said. "I think I could handle this very well." She paused, knowing the sensitive questions were coming. "What I don't know if I could handle is the salary and benefits."

Nadine smiled. "I don't blame you for your concern." She slid a second sheet across to Karen. "Our board is excited about the position, and our benefactors are supporting this need. You won't be rich, but I hope it's something you can live on."

Karen studied the sheet. The salary was lower than she'd been earning, but the insurance looked good, as did the leave days for vacation and illness. She lifted her gaze to Nadine's questioning eyes and nodded. "I can live with this, too."

"God be praised," Nadine said. "We've had two other applicants. I've spoken with one, and I have another interview at the end of the week. I'll take the information to the board as soon as I can, and I'll let you know. I'm sure they'll want to interview our first choice. . .but then, maybe not."

Karen rose, feeling hopeful.

"By the way, I have something for you." Nadine rummaged through her in and out box and pulled out an envelope. She handed it to Karen. "This came a couple of days ago. I figured I could give it to you today."

"Thank you," Karen said, feeling a frown settle on her face as she studied the envelope. She eyed the return address and saw the name Ada Reynolds.

Clutching the envelope, Karen said good-bye, and when she stepped outside, she sent a thank you to the Lord for heading her in this direction. If the board selected her, Karen felt confident they would do so with God's blessings.

She clasped the letter in her hand and didn't open it until she'd started the car and turned on the air-conditioning. Praying the woman was well and having no serious problems, Karen tore open the envelope. She scanned the letter as tears filled her eyes.

Dear Karen,

Thank you so much for your kindness to my children. You gave them many fun-filled hours with new experiences they will never forget.

I'm sure you know that we are back at home and safe from my husband's wrath. My faith was strong during that time at My Friend's Place, but I want you to know that your example of God's love and compassion gave me courage. I have tried to be a forgiving woman, but seeing the joy in my children's faces when they returned from visits with you, hearing the freedom they had running through the meadow and singing in the trees, I realized that we had no freedom with an abusive man. Until he opens his heart to God's bidding and loves us as the Bible commands, our lives are in danger and without fulfillment. Having you in our lives made a difference. I was able to do what I did to protect my children.

Thank you also for sharing your faith with Hailey and Dylan. They returned to the facility singing songs about Jesus, and this gave me such comfort. I pray the Lord guides your life in the ways He wants you to go. I pray that you are washed in God's blessings.

In His love,
Ada Reynolds

Karen let her tears flow. They ran down her cheeks and dripped on her suit jacket. Leaning her head against the steering wheel, she closed her eyes and praised God for giving her an opportunity to witness for Him and the joy of touching lives that made a difference.

She spoke the amen aloud, then shuffled through her purse for a tissue. After she wiped away her tears, a smile settled on her face. God is in the heavens and all is right with the world.

fifteen

Karen slid on her jeans and an old T-shirt. She needed to pick apples because Gramma Bea had promised to continue the pie-baking lessons so she would be prepared for the Arts and Apple Fest the coming weekend.

Perspiration beaded Karen's hairline as she headed down the staircase. Autumn had taken a step back the past few days and decided to reissue the summer's heat. Today promised to be another scorcher. The scent of coffee greeted her as she reached the bottom step. Her grandfather's coffee was always an adventure, but today it smelled rich and fresh, the way she liked it. Still, she knew a taste test was necessary before she'd drink a full cup.

Her grandfather sat at the kitchen table. He'd pushed his empty plate aside. He seemed content, but his face looked pale. Concern skittered up Karen's spine.

"Not feeling well?"

"It's the heat," he said. "I was restless all night."

She watched him raise his hand to his chest and press against his heart. Her fear deepened. "You need to get air-conditioning in this house, Grandpa. The Kendalls have it." She slammed her mouth closed, realizing she'd opened an unwelcome topic.

"He gives no money to the church so he can afford air-conditioning. I tithe."

Karen shook her head. She knew her grandfather had enough money for his own unit, but he had to put down the Kendalls one way or the other. She elected not to respond.

"Only good thing that came out of that family, besides

Bea, is that young man who hangs around here. At least he has a brain, and we saw him in church."

"Eric's a Christian, Grandpa."

Her grandfather's hand hadn't left his chest, and being subtle about it made no sense. "Are you having chest pains?"

He lowered his hand. "I'm fine."

"You're holding your chest like something's wrong."

"Can't a man do what he wants in his house without someone judging every move?"

Karen gave up and pulled out a bowl. She added cereal and fruit then sat beside her grandfather. "I'm going out to pick apples today. Tomorrow I'm making lots of pies with Gramma Bea."

"I'll give you a hand at pickin'," he said. He drained his cup then rose for another.

"It's too hot, Grandpa. I want you to stay inside today. Sit on the back porch in the shade. Hopefully you'll get a breeze there."

"You telling me what to do again?" He gave her a gruff look.

Karen knew this was her grandpa's way. "Yes. I'm taking Grandma's place and telling you what to do."

He waved his hand at her as if her words could be brushed away, but she hoped he listened. When she finished her breakfast, she set her dishes in the dishwasher. "I forgot my hat," she said.

She left her grandfather and headed back upstairs in search of her straw hat. It had been her grandmother's, and Karen had found it shortly after her arrival. The hat not only held many memories, it would serve a useful purpose on this hot day.

She found it on a hook in her closet and slapped it on her head. She glanced in the mirror and chuckled. As she descended the steps again, the telephone rang. By the third jingle, she knew her grandfather wasn't going to answer, so she bolted down the last few steps and caught it.

"Karen?" the voice said.

"Yes, this is Karen," she said while catching her breath.

"It didn't sound like you. This is Nadine."

Karen's chest tightened. "Hi, Nadine. I was out of breath. Any news?" She waited anxiously.

"No news, but I wanted to let you know that I feel positive about things. The last interview didn't go well, and your credentials seem to top them both. I'm meeting with the board on Monday, so we should have some news very soon after that."

Karen let out a pent-up breath. "Thanks for letting me know. I've been wondering."

"I've been praying," Nadine said. "No matter what, we can count on the Lord."

Karen smiled. "Yes, we can."

After her good-bye, she hung up the telephone then went to the kitchen to check on her grandfather. She was concerned why he hadn't answered. When she stepped through the doorway, she knew why. He wasn't there. She poured a thermos of water then went in search of him. "Where are you?" she called.

He didn't answer.

"Grandpa?"

No response. She couldn't find him on the lower floors. An uneasy feeling caused her to ascend the steps again to the second story. No Grandpa. Fear gripped her. Where was he? The half bath downstairs perhaps. She hadn't noticed him there, but it was a possibility. She descended the stairs two at a time, careened around the corner, and stopped. The bathroom door stood open. She hurried to the back porch again. Maybe she'd missed him.

The porch stood empty. Karen headed through the doorway, her gaze like a beacon, shifting back and forth, but she caught no sight of him. When she looked in the shed, the dolly stood against the wall and baskets sat on the tables. Then she noticed a small cart missing. The truth struck her. He'd gone to the orchard in spite of what she'd said.

Karen loaded the dolly with baskets, tossed in the thermos and tugged it all through the doorway. She hurried along the meadow path while the empty baskets pitched and bumped on the dolly. When she drew closer to the orchard, she could see her grandfather high on a ladder. He wore a burlap sack strapped around his neck, and she could see him lowering the apples into the bag. Her prayer rose as she closed the distance.

"Why are you up there?" she called from below. "I asked you to stay inside today."

"I didn't want to," he said. "I always picked apples for your grandmother's pies for the booth. I'm not stopping now."

Her heart wrenched with his words. She could only imagine how much he missed his wife. How could she stop him from doing something so important? Her wisdom fought her emotions, but her heart won the battle.

Karen walked away and grabbed an empty bushel, then headed down the row until she found a tree with ripe apples hanging from the lower branches. She plucked them from the limb and set them into the basket. The heat beat down through the trees, and she paused to take a drink from the thermos. She was certain her grandfather would be thirsty, too.

She left her basket and started down the row toward her grandfather. When she came through the trees, she noticed he wasn't on the ladder. She looked below. He wasn't there, either. Her feet carried her like the wind, and as she rounded the dolly, she found her grandfather sprawled on the ground.

Fear stabbed her, and tears raced to her eyes. "Grandpa!"

He didn't move.

"Lord, please, help him," she cried. She knelt at his side and saw the faint rise of his chest. He was alive. "Grandpa!"

He didn't move, not an eye blink.

Karen dropped the thermos beside him and sprinted through the trees to the meadow. She needed help. She needed Eric. She veered around her own picket fence and raced to the back of the Kendalls'. "Eric!" She pounded on the door.

No sound came from inside.

"Help, please!" she called.

Then she heard sounds, but instead of Eric, Lionel Kendall came to the back door, his face in a deep frown.

"What's all the noise?" He pushed the door back. "Eric's not home. He's at his store."

Her heart sank to her toes. "Grandpa's in the orchard. He needs help."

"Walter?" His frown changed to fear.

Karen had no time to question Lionel's mood or his expression. Her grandfather could be dying. "He's unconscious, but he seems to be breathing. Please. He needs help."

"Use the phone and call 911 while I go and see what I can do."

His last words faded away as he darted across the backyard and into the meadow.

Karen had never seen Eric's grandfather move that quickly. Amazed, she bounded into the house and dialed for help. When she'd given the information, she tore through the doorway and headed back to the orchard.

The heat shimmered off the timothy and tall grasses, now dried from the summer sun, and they tangled around her legs as she ran. When she arrived her heart stopped. Her grandfather was sitting on the dolly drinking from the thermos that Lionel was holding to his lips.

"Grandpa," she cried, racing to his side. "What happened?"

He shook his head. "Last I knew I was climbing down the ladder with a bag full of apples."

"The heat," Lionel said. He aimed a disbelieving look at her grandfather. "You, old codger, don't have a lick of sense."

"You ought to know, Lionel. You left your brain out in the rain, and it shrunk."

"Stop this." Karen's voice rose through the trees frightening the birds. They fluttered from the branches into the sky. Both men halted in mid barbs and gaped at her.

"That's enough from both of you. You've been neighbors forever and friends, too. It's time you acted like men and not little boys." She saw shock on their faces. "I'm sorry, but it's the truth."

She turned toward Lionel. "Thanks so much for your help. Do you think we can get Grandpa up to the house for the EMS."

"EMS," her grandfather said, his face settling into a new scowl. "Now why in the good earth did you call them?"

Karen's fist punched against her hip. "Because you were unconscious on the ground, and your neighbor told me to." She motioned toward Lionel.

"Trying to keep me alive, are you?" her grandfather asked Lionel. "I suppose life wouldn't be as interesting without me to taunt."

"Hush up, old man, and rest yourself on that dolly," Lionel said. "I'm pulling you back to the house."

"Like snow in summer, you are." Walter struggled to rise, but Karen pushed him back and lifted his feet. He finally gave up as the dolly jiggled onto the pathway.

Karen followed, hearing her grandfather carry on that Lionel was trying to break his back or rattle his brain loose. She didn't hear his response, but she was certain Eric's grandfather asked, "Who said he had a brain?"

≈

Eric rapped on the screen door then called. He heard Karen's voice in the distance and stepped inside. She met him in the living room, exhaustion straining her expression.

He opened his arms, and she fell into them, tears warming

his chest where they soaked through his shirt.

"Is he all right?" Eric asked, pressing his cheek against her herbal-scented hair.

"Heat and stress, they said. They decided not to keep him in the emergency room, so he's home." Karen tilted her teary face toward him. "Sorry for messing up your shirt."

"You didn't mess my shirt, so don't be sorry. I couldn't believe what Gramma told me when I got back. She'd been away to the church for a Bible study, and she came back in time to see the EMS pulling into your driveway. She said her heart was in her throat."

"Mine, too. You can't imagine how awful it was."

They settled together on the sofa. He listened as she told him the details, and he was amazed at what he heard. "I thank the Lord your grandfather's okay, and I'm praising God for the change."

"What change?"

"You said my granddad ran into the orchard to save your grandfather's life. Now that's change, and if it's not God's handiwork, I don't know what is."

"I was so upset the thought didn't occur to me. How could I have missed that?" Her smile widened. "The Lord heard our prayers."

"Maybe this is the beginning of a new relationship for them."

"Maybe, and speaking of prayers, I heard from Nadine today."

His heart lurched. "You got the job."

"No, but it's looking good. She said mine was the best interview. The meeting with the board is Monday, and she'll call me as soon as she hears their decision."

He grasped her hands in his. "Then I won't stop praying for you. I'm really pleased, Karen. I think you'll be content working there."

"I think so, too, and I'll be closer to Grandpa. He needs family nearby."

"He takes chances, too, like going out to pick apples alone." Eric's mind shifted. "So what about the apples?"

Her eyebrows lifted. "I forgot about those. We have some in the shed, but Grandpa and I both had a partial bushel in the orchard. I suppose I should go back and finish the job."

"*We* should go back," he corrected. He stood and drew her upward. When they reached the yard, Eric grasped the dolly handle, and they walked side by side back into the orchard.

When they reached the thermos and apple-filled burlap sack, Eric pictured his ornery grandfather standing over Walter Chapman, concerned about his life. The picture warmed his heart, as did the woman standing beside him. God had worked many miracles in the past weeks, and Eric felt certain he should leave things in the Lord's hands.

With the sweet scent of ripe apples on the air, Eric stood beside the woman who'd changed his life in so many ways as he plucked the rosy fruit from the branches. An apple had caused the world to fall into sin, but Eric knew that these apples were bringing him closer to the kind of love God had in store for all of His children.

ॐ

Karen watched Gramma Bea dust the counter with flour and deftly roll out the dough. She placed it into a pie tin, then heaped in the sliced apples, which had been mixed with sugar and flour. Karen daubed on the butter while Eric's grandmother rolled the top crust.

"It looks so easy when you do it," Karen said.

"Next time, it's your turn." Gramma Bea gave her a warm smile and finished crimping the edge.

Karen's turn came, and she followed directions. This time the flour kept the dough where it was supposed to be, and when Karen lifted it, the circle of pastry rose easily from the countertop. She placed it into the pie tin then Gramma Bea filled it with the apple mixture. The top crust rolled as smoothly as the bottom. Karen couldn't help but smile as she took her turn crimping the edge. She'd made a pretty good-looking pie.

They worked side by side pulling pies from the oven to the cooling racks and starting again. Karen enjoyed the Kendalls' air conditioner, and even with that luxury, the oven warmed the room. Her cheeks felt hot, and she figured they were as rosy as a new apple.

Karen began a new batch of dough. She'd watched the older woman work the shortening into the flour in small pea-sized nuggets, then gently add the liquid, making sure not to overwork the dough. She felt for the familiar consistency and was satisfied. She liked what she felt.

As she began the next crust, Karen took a chance on opening an unwanted door. "I was looking at some of my grandmother's old photographs the other day. I didn't know Eric's grandfather and mine were friends years ago." She paused a moment to watch Gramma Bea's expression.

Her face didn't flinch. "They were good friends for most of their childhood. Even in high school. They were inseparable." She gave Karen a curious look.

Inseparable? That seemed utterly impossible. Karen paused, then decided that since she'd taken one step forward, why not go for two? "So what happened? I can't imagine anything ruining such a strong friendship."

She hesitated then released a long breath. Whatever she'd kept private for so many years appeared ready to be released. Though Karen should have felt victory, instead she felt like a traitor.

Gramma Bea gave Karen a tender smile. "It's all so ridiculous. You know men. They're competitive. They can't give up until they win, and Lionel's the worst. He hates to lose."

"Competitive? Over what?"

As she asked the question, her Grandmother Hazel's voice rang in her ears. "Lionel was a poor loser."

Her chest tightened. "Maybe I shouldn't have asked."

Gramma Bea patted Karen's hand with her floured fingers, leaving a white imprint. "You're welcome to ask. Just don't try to make sense out of it." She turned her attention to the pies as she talked. "It's just so silly, it's not worth the breath."

Karen waited, longing to know the truth.

"During high school," she began, "your Grandma and Lionel were best of friends. Though nothing had been said while they were young, Lionel had planned to ask Hazel to marry him one day."

"Mr. Kendall and my grandmother?" Karen's pulse skipped as her thoughts flew back to the photographs and her grandfather's reaction. Things began falling into place.

"Yep, that's what he thought, but your grandma was a strong Christian woman"—she gave Karen a grin—"and you know Lionel. He's a believer all right, but he only sets his feet in church for special occasions. I've known him to go on Christmas and Easter. Weddings and funerals. Not much more. But he does read his Bible."

Hearing that he read Scripture made Karen feel much better.

"So getting back to the story," Gramma Bea said, "when the relationship grew more serious with Lionel, Hazel began to have second thoughts. Maybe her parents said they were unequally yoked. Maybe she realized that sitting in church alone for the rest of her life wasn't what she wanted."

Karen listened, her pulse racing with the information.

"Anyway, your grandfather always showed respect for their relationship until Hazel's eyes turned toward him more and more often."

"Grandma was a flirt, I think."

"She was, but in an acceptable sense of the word. She enjoyed life and was playful. Fun to be with and very honest."

"So Grandpa captured her heart."

"Yes, I'd say so." Gramma Bea chuckled. "Lionel didn't let

water flow under the bridge for very long. He and I knew each other, too, and within a few weeks Hazel was only a distant memory. Lionel's aunt lived close to my house, and suddenly he appeared in my neighborhood more and more. He'd drop by for a visit, and soon we'd fallen in love. We married and lived in a little apartment until his parents moved to Arizona for their health. Then we moved here—right next door to Hazel and Walter."

"And the feud began," Karen said.

"Not *began*. The foolishness continued," Gramma Bea corrected. "They'd long gotten over the issue of Walter marrying your grandmother. It became a game of one-upmanship. They were like two little boys trying to get the best of each other. They both acted like blockheads to me."

Karen laughed at Gramma Bea's description. "I think the same." She finished another pie and moved to the next, amazed at how fast she worked when distracted. "What amazed me was when Mr. Kendall came to my grandfather's help yesterday."

"You see. That's why they're so silly." Gramma Bea rested her hand on the countertop and shook her head. "I really think they feel like brothers, but they're just too proud to give in."

"I can't believe it's dragged on this long over nothing. Eric and I have talked about this a lot, and we plan to fix everything," Karen said. "Just you wait."

sixteen

Standing inside the pie booth, Karen wiped the perspiration from her forehead with a tissue and tucked it into her pocket. She couldn't believe how many pies they'd sold. Some of the women would bring theirs later in the afternoon so pies were arriving fresh throughout the day. The fund-raiser had been a tremendous success.

"Getting tired?" Gramma Bea asked, dropping by the booth.

"A little. It's hot, and the sun's been beating on us, but it's moved now."

"You should take a break. I think Mrs. Russell will be here to replace you in a few minutes. She glanced at the sheet of paper she'd pulled from her pocket. "Yes. She should take over any minute." She gestured toward the other booths. "You haven't had a chance to look around at all the crafts and food booths."

Karen felt her stomach grumble. Being in charge, she'd felt a responsibility to stick around, but Gramma Bea had truly been the leader, and Karen felt grateful. "I am starving. I've been staring at these pies all afternoon. What I'd love is a tall glass of lemonade or even apple cider." Cider? Why had she agreed to look at anything related to apples? She'd seen too many lately.

"I'll run to get you something, and as I said, Mrs. Russell should be here in a minute."

Gramma Bea moved off, and Karen took a moment's reprieve to rest. She sank into the chair behind the counter, leaned back, and closed her eyes. The sun sent a rosy glow through her eyelids until something blocked the light.

"Apple Annie's tired?"

She jerked upward, hearing Eric's voice. "Where have you been all day?"

"At the building. It's looking good." He handed her a large drink in a plastic tumbler.

She couldn't help but smile, seeing the excitement on his face. She grasped the container and took a long sip. Lemonade. Her cheeks puckered to its welcome tartness.

"I ran into Gramma. She told me where you were and gave me your drink order."

"Thanks." She toasted him with another swallow. "I'm really happy to hear about the building."

"I'm so anxious, anticipating the completion. I feel like a kid waiting to unwrap the gifts his parents have hidden on the floor of their closet."

"Is that where your parents hid them?" Karen remembered her mother kept theirs in the attic.

His eyes sparkled. "You guessed it."

As he spoke the last word, a woman strode to the booth with a smile. "Hi, I'm Wilma Russell. Ready for a break?"

"I sure am," Karen said. She took a moment to explain the procedure then joined Eric on the customer side of the booth. "Someone else should be with you soon. We decided to double up on help later in the day."

The woman gave them a wave, and Eric linked his arm with hers as they moved toward the other activities at the festival. Karen stopped to gaze at a homemade birdhouse and a hand-woven rug. The scent of roasted sausages, burgers, and popcorn hovered on the air as they maneuvered past the crowded aisles between the booths. After they'd had enough of handcrafted gifts, apple and fruit preserves, candy apples, apples of all kinds sold by the peck, face painting, and fake tattoos, Eric stopped beside a food booth.

"How about a hot dog?" Eric asked.

She agreed, and with her hot dog in hand, they moved

into the shade. The Pigeon River gurgled beyond the trees, and Eric led her closer through some taller grass where they sat on the bank and ate their snack. He opened a bag of potato chips and held them out for her. She nibbled one, feeling as if nothing could be more wonderful than sitting in the grass beside him.

"I have some news for you," he said, breaking the silence.

She faced him, noting a special tone in his voice, as if he'd solved the world's problems. "Something good, I hope."

"I hope." He bit into another chip then took a sip of his lemonade. "How's this for a solution to the farmer quandary? It's not perfect, but I think it's better than doing nothing."

She sat straighter, realizing he'd given this so much thought, not for himself, but for her concern for the farmers. The awareness touched. her. "I can't wait," she said.

"What if I give farmers the option of selling their own produce on consignment at little stands within the store. The products could be tagged with a special bar code so they would receive their rightful cut of the sale. Those who don't want to sell the products themselves can have the choice of selling the produce directly to me. I'll have a special locally homegrown section."

She tried to imagine how that might work. "It's great, if you think that's not too complicated."

"I picture small stands right inside the front doors where farmers can sell their wares in any weather. In winter, when their produce is gone, I could hire those interested to work with the produce inside the market, bag groceries, and any other jobs that come along. This will provide a little added income even in the winter months."

"That's a great idea, Eric. People so often give the jobs to high school students and forget the senior citizens."

"That's what I was thinking. They'll have a chance to be with people, keep vital, and have a purpose. Some may not be interested, but people like your grandfather might enjoy it."

She reached out and wrapped both arms around his neck. "You are one of the kindest, sweetest people I know. If this doesn't work, it's not that you didn't try. You're a very special man."

He rested his hands on her shoulders and looked into her eyes. "You're a very special woman. Do you think that's why the Lord decided for us to meet again after our youthful encounter in the cornrows?"

She chuckled at the memory. "Could be." Her own news grabbed her. "I have some news for you, too."

"The job?" Interest filled his face and his eyes searched hers.

"No. Something more personal." She braced herself against the ground to rise. "Let's walk for a while."

Eric leaped up to help her rise, while a curious look covered his face.

Karen stood and brushed the back of her pants, then for the first time, she took the initiative and reached for Eric's hand.

He gave her a tender look as they moved off together along the river.

"What's your news?" he asked. "I sense it's something important."

"It is, and I'm luxuriating in the information."

"You're teasing me. Getting even is what I'd call it for all the times I taunted you." He drew her closer and nuzzled his cheek against her hair. "Come on. Tell me."

She tilted her head upward. "Well. . .I know it wasn't a pig that caused the feud."

He looked surprised. "What do you mean? Did you find out something?" His eyes widened, and an earnest look covered his face.

"I know how it started."

"How did you find out? Who told you? Why didn't you tell me earlier?"

He asked one question after another until Karen had to shush him. "I asked Gramma Bea, and she finally gave up the silence. She told me the story."

"She told you? Tell me."

She grinned at his impatience, but she didn't blame him. Karen told him the story just as she'd heard it from Gramma Bea. Eric's comments echoed her own while she'd listened to the tale, and when she finished, they stood grinning at each other, amazed that the mystery had been solved.

"If we had known, we should have pleaded Psalm 79 to the Lord."

Eric tilted his head. "Sorry. I don't know Bible verses by heart."

"I only remember some, but here's the one I mean. 'Do not hold against us the sins of the fathers; may your mercy come quickly to meet us, for we are in desperate need.'"

"And we were desperate," Eric said, "except you got part of that wrong."

"Wrong?"

"It was the sins of the grandfathers."

"It was."

The river rippled past, mixing their chuckles with its bubbling sound.

"We've come a long way in a short time," Eric said, slipping his arm around her shoulder, then paused, his eyes filled with tenderness. "I hope you feel as I do, Karen."

Her heart jolted, and she studied his face. How did he feel? "I'm not certain what you're thinking, Eric."

"Then I'll tell you, but do you really want to hear this?"

She nodded and held her breath.

"I believe that God has worked wonders in our lives. He's brought us back together—old friends, of sorts, meeting again. He's brought about job changes. Today I'm almost the owner of a specialty market, and you're nearly the public relations person for a women's shelter."

"Dreams came true for both of us," Karen said, squeezing his hand.

"For sure. And the Lord has brought us closer to our families. I'll be back in Gaylord nearer my grandparents, and if this job comes through—and I think it will—you'll be moving nearby, too."

"Probably in with Grandpa until I make other arrangements."

Eric halted and drew her into his arms. They stood face-to-face beside the riverbank. Karen looked into his eyes and saw so many words yet to be spoken.

Eric leaned closer and brushed his lips against hers. "I can offer you some other arrangements."

"Other arrangements?" His meaning didn't register.

"Living arrangements," he said.

She drew back, afraid of what she was hearing. "Eric, I would never—"

"Karen, no." His face paled. "I'm not proposing anything inappropriate. When a man and woman get married, they live in the same house."

"Get married?" The sound of the river hummed in her ears, and she clung to him, unable to believe what he had said.

Dismay and shock flashed to his face. "You don't feel as I do?"

His expression broke her heart.

"I love you, Karen. I thought you understood that, but I was afraid to move too quickly for fear—"

"Never fear," Karen said. "I do feel the same. I think I fell in love with you when I was sitting in that tree, but I didn't want to admit it."

"In the tree?"

"Maybe not that soon, but a long time ago." She smiled, and his face gleamed like sunshine.

"I know this is what God wants," Eric said. "I know it's what I want. We don't have to rush. We'll take time to get to know each other better and to adjust to our new careers."

"You're that confident in me?"

He brushed his finger across her cheek. "I have all the confidence in the world in you. . .and in the Lord who led us to each other."

Karen knew Eric was right. When she finally quit fighting the Lord, He took charge and made all things right. One problem still rose to her mind. "We still have work to do, though."

He seemed to know what she meant and smiled. "The answer is in the Bible," Karen said. " 'If you hold anything against anyone, forgive him, so that your Father in heaven may forgive you your sins.' It's time our grandfathers ask for forgiveness. We know they like each other. Look what happened when my granddad was unconscious in the orchard."

"You're right," he said.

"You ready to go out on a limb with me one more time?" she asked.

"Real limb or figurative?"

"Maybe both, but I'm talking about setting up a plan that'll force those two to shake hands. They have to, if we're going to be together."

Eric nestled her against his chest. "I'll go out on a limb with you anytime."

❧

Karen hung up the telephone and clapped her hands together. Nadine had called to say the job was hers. Her first instinct was to thank the Lord for His loving guidance. Her second thought was Eric. She punched in the numbers and listened to the telephone ring. When Gramma Bea answered, she asked for Eric and waited.

His voice came over the line, and Karen let out a whoop.

"What is it?" he asked, sounding as if he wasn't sure if she were happy or dying.

"Nadine called. I've been hired for the position."

"I knew it," he said, his voice reflecting her joy. "Now what do you have to do? You're still employed by the other agency."

"I'll give my notice when I get back. It'll give me time to pack my belongings and get out of my apartment lease."

"And I'll be here waiting for you."

"I'm not that far away. We'll see each other. I can come up on weekends."

He chuckled into the phone. "I guess you're right. What's three hours?"

"Nothing where love's involved," she said. "Now the job gives me a great reason for inviting Grandpa on the picnic we talked about."

"Are you going to tell him about the new job?"

"Yes, but not where it is. I'll save that for the picnic. Have you said anything to your grandparents yet?"

"I did today. I told them I want to take them to see the store, and then we're going out to eat. The picnic part will be a surprise."

"You're a chicken," she said. "They probably hate picnics."

He laughed. "Just Granddad, but he'll get over it. I love you, Karen, with all my heart."

"Me, too," she said.

When she disconnected, she took a deep breath. Life was amazing. A few weeks had made all the difference in the world. Not only had she fallen in love, but she also had a new job and a great plan to heal a long-standing grudge.

"Grandpa," she said, hurrying to the back porch. "Guess what. I've just heard I've been hired for a new job. I thought we could celebrate. How about going on a picnic tomorrow?"

seventeen

Karen opened the trunk and pulled out the picnic basket. She handed it to her grandfather while he eyed her with suspicion. He'd asked numerous times why the two of them were going on a picnic. She gave him a variety of answers. He accepted none.

She lifted out a small cooler, then lowered the lid, and led the way to the banks of the Manistee River. Picnic benches sat beneath the colorful trees, and being a weekday, the park was quiet, the way she and Eric had hoped it would be.

When she placed the cooler on the bench, she returned to the car for two canvas chairs. She knew her grandfather would grumble about having to sit too long on a picnic bench.

"It's a beautiful day," she said, trying to pass the time until Eric arrived, but the afternoon was unbelievable—almost perfect. The bright blue sky was feathered with wisps of gentle clouds. A breeze fluttered through the trees, shaking the crisp leaves. Some broke from the limbs and drifted down like orange and gold butterflies flitting to the ground. The humidity had lowered, with a temperature in the seventies. She felt a hint of autumn in the air. Seasons changed, and so did lives. She, Eric, and their grandparents would have so much to look forward to after things settled.

She'd prayed hard all night long, each time she woke, asking God to guide the day and bring about a gentle peace between the grandfathers. She prayed, too, that she and Eric would use their time well to get to know each other and adjust to the many changes they would face. Though she prayed for the Lord's continued blessing, Karen felt certain God would continue to direct her and Eric's path.

Silence lengthened between them.

"What do you say, Grandpa?"

"I say let's eat so I can get back home. I don't like eating with ants or any bug, for that matter."

Karen ignored his grumbles and opened a canvas chair. "Here. Sit in the comfortable seat, and let's enjoy the quiet. We don't get to do that too often." She filled her lungs. "Smell the fresh air. It's nice."

Her grandfather sat, then squirmed in the lawn chair and studied her with narrowed eyes. "You have something up your sleeve, Karen. I just don't know what it is."

You'll know soon enough, she thought. She patted his hand and drew her chair up beside his. "Let's talk."

"Talk?"

She nodded.

"About what? You need a loan?" His steady gaze looked suspicious.

"I don't need a loan. I want to talk about you. How are you feeling?"

"Good," he said. "Better when I'm in my recliner."

"Grandpa, you're hopeless." She leaned closer. "I worry about you. About your health and your loneliness. I hope the time I've spent with you has been nice. I have to go back to the city next week."

Her grandfather's back straightened, and his eyes glinted as if he'd gained some understanding. "So that's it. You're worried about your old grandfather."

He leaned forward and grasped her hand. "I'll be fine, Karen. Losing your grandmother was like having my arm cut off. It takes time to learn to use the other one. I loved having you here, but you have a life, and I can't interfere. I'd love you to live closer. You've been a special granddaughter to me, but we don't always get what we like. We settle for what's necessary."

She nodded, wanting so badly to tell him the surprise.

"I'm glad. When I'm gone, I want you to remember that you need to rest and not push yourself. No more climbing apple trees in the heat. Hire some young whippersnapper to do that for you."

He chuckled at her *whippersnapper* phrase.

Before she said more, she heard a car pull onto the gravel. The motor stopped, and she turned toward the parking lot. Her pulse skipped as she saw Eric climb from the car.

Her grandfather had noticed the sound, too, and chuckled. "So that young man's followed you here." But his voice faded to silence when he saw Lionel Kendall climb from the passenger seat.

Eric opened the back door, and his grandmother slid out. Together, they carried their picnic gear onto the grass while all tension hung on the air until Lionel spotted her grandfather.

"What's this?" he roared. "It's a plot."

"Hush up, you old bag of wind," Walter yelled back.

Eric put his hand on his grandfather's shoulder and said something that quieted him.

Karen watched her grandfather's face grow curious as he followed their every step.

"Hi, Gramma Bea," Karen said, kissing her on the cheek. She nodded to Eric's grandfather, whose face looked as if it had been caught in a vise.

"Everyone sit down," Eric said. "We're having a picnic whether you like it or not, but before we eat, Karen and I have some things to tell you."

Heads swiveled from one to the other. Grumbles sounded from their grandfathers, but Eric stood his ground, and soon the three grandparents had settled into their lawn chairs, their gazes glued to Eric.

"First, we're going to deal with this ridiculous, eternal squabbling." He turned to his grandfather. "Granddad, do you love Gramma?"

The old man drew back and gawked at Eric like he was on the brink of insanity. "What do you think? We've been married for nearly fifty years."

"Gramma, how about you?" he asked.

She gave a chuckle. "I'd be out of mind to stick with him if I didn't love him. Who wants to wake up each day to a grouchy old man who thinks of every childish thing in the book to do to his neighbor?"

"Beatrice!" Lionel swiveled and frowned at his wife, while his cheeks flushed.

"Don't blame her, Grandpa. How do you think the Lord feels with all this foolish squabbling? You've been holding a grudge all these years over which one of you two married Hazel?"

Lionel's back drew upward as straight as a plumb line. "Who told you that?"

"It's a fact. You've been a poor loser, and worst of all, you don't really care."

"Phooey! This has nothing to do with who married Hazel. That was long ago. It's the principle of the thing," Lionel said, pointing to Walter. "He always had to have the last word. Always had to come out on top. I just got tired of it."

Karen touched her grandfather's arm, afraid he'd yell something back. Instead, he leaned forward and shook his head. "You've won the big one, Lionel."

Eric's grandfather drew back. "What are you talking about?"

"We both were winners when it came to marriage. The Lord led the four of us to each other, and we both had wonderful marriages until Hazel died. You and Bea still have many good years ahead. I'd say you came out the winner."

Lionel paused a moment, his mouth hanging open like a Venus's-flytrap. He glanced at Gramma Bea, then Eric, and then Karen before his gaze settled on her grandfather.

"Walter, you're breaking my heart," Lionel said. "I know you miss Hazel. After she died, I held Bea in my arms at night and felt tears in my eyes, knowing how lonely you must be. The feud just seemed to go on, and it got such a habit I didn't know when to stop."

"Neither did I," Walter said. "Guess we made dolts out of ourselves with our foolishness." His pause grew until he chuckled. "I was always amazed at what you could come up with."

"You're pretty ingenious yourself," Lionel said. "I know I'm not a good Christian. I should go to church. I'm just a lazy man, but Bea's told me over and over I had to stop. I just didn't know how to let the feud die gracefully."

Eric put his arm around his grandfather's shoulder. "You know Karen and I have strong feelings for each other, and you two arguing made it hard for us to know how we really felt. We've been praying for this to stop, and we thank God it has."

"We have more news, too," Karen said, giving Eric a nod. "You go first."

Eric detailed his idea to help the farmers in the community. Though Lionel didn't sell produce, Karen watched her grandfather's face brighten as Eric talked.

Walter clapped his hands. "You mean you'll hire me to bag groceries and kibitz with the customers?"

"I sure will," Eric said, his face beaming.

"What about those teenagers?" He eyed Karen. "Those whippersnappers who always get those jobs?"

"They'll have to look elsewhere. I'm employing the old codgers."

Everyone laughed, even Eric's grandfather.

"You've done a nice thing," Walter said. "I can still do my stand if I want and still sell my produce at your market. The best of both worlds."

Eric agreed. "Now it's your turn, Karen."

A lump formed in Karen's throat as she looked at her grandfather. "I'm leaving at the end of the week, but I'll be back."

Her grandfather's face shifted from attentive to perplexed.

"I'm going home to give my notice at the agency and to pack my belongings."

"Your belongings? Why?" His face sagged. "Where are you moving?"

Karen rose and wrapped her arm around her grandfather's neck. "I have a job here in Gaylord. I'll begin in a month, so I'm facing lots of changes. I hope you won't mind if I stay with you for a while." The job details could wait. Right now, his delight was most important.

"Mind? You're kidding. I'd be happy as a pig in mud," Walter said.

"But she can only live with you temporarily," Eric added.

"Temporarily." Walter paused and pinched his lower lip. "Right. Karen'll want her own place, I'm sure."

"Not her own place," Eric said. "She'll be moving in with me."

Heads turned into swizzle sticks as they gazed back and forth, with eyebrows raised.

Eric chuckled. "Stop your worrying. We have good news."

Karen shifted to stand beside Eric. He slid his fingers between hers and raised her hand to his lips with a kiss. She watched the grandparents' faces shift from confusion to smiles.

"We've fallen in love." He held up his hand to hold back their comments. "Since this has been a fast courtship, we're not making any plans right now. Karen will live here with you, and we'll have a chance to get to know each other better. We're putting this in God's hands, but we both feel that the Lord has guided our paths to each other."

"Eric kissed me years ago in the cornrows. We were only children then, but we truly believe that God has brought us back together for His purpose."

Eric squeezed her hand and turned her to face him. "Now I have a surprise for you."

Her heart tripped in her chest. "For me?" She had no idea

what he had in store for her. She held her breath.

Eric shifted in front of her and went down on one knee. He slipped his hand in his pocket and pulled out a velvet-covered box.

Karen's pulse raced while her heart thudded in her chest.

"Karen, you've given me such joy. You've strengthened my faith and shown me how God must be the center of my life. I've known of you for years, and now I want to know you better so our future can be side by side. Will you honor me by being my wife?"

Her hand trembled as she accepted the box. Thoughts tumbled in her head. Yes, she'd known that marriage was in store for them, but she had no idea he would ask her today or that he would offer her the token of his love. She lifted the lid and her hands shook with such extreme that Eric chuckled and pulled the ring from the slot.

It glittered sparks of fire in the sunshine. The beautiful diamond sat in a gold setting. Eric slid the ring on her finger and looked into her eyes. "Will you?" he asked.

"You know I will," she said, resting her arms around his neck and gazing into his wonderful, smiling face.

He drew her closer and kissed her lightly on the lips. When they parted, Karen turned her attention to their grandparents, who had bundled together like the best of friends—shaking hands and hugging.

Her grandfather captured her in his arms with a bear hug then stepped away to shake Eric's hand. Eric's grandparents followed. Lionel hugged her close and whispered how happy he was, and Gramma Bea, whose eyes were filled with tears, clasped her to her chest with blessings.

"Let's eat," Walter said.

The group laughed then went about setting out the picnic food. After the blessing, they delved in, and when everyone was full and the food was put away, Eric clasped Karen's hand.

"We're going for a short walk if you don't mind," he said.

"Mind?" Gramma Bea said. "You two deserve time alone. Have fun."

Eric's spirit lifted when he took Karen's hand and led her away from their grandparents' eyes. They wandered along the riverbank then stopped beneath a large sprawling oak. "We're alone."

Her eyes sparkled as brightly as the ring on her finger. "We are."

"I wanted a few minutes alone to tell you how much I love you. I knew when Janine and I split that God had something special in store for me. I felt it in my heart as well as knew it in my head. Then you walked into my life. . . ." He chuckled, recalling the moment. "You didn't quite walk in. You hovered above me on a tree limb then hobbled away, but that day I sensed something special. I asked my grandmother about you as soon as I got back to the house."

"What did you ask? 'Who could the goofy girl be sitting in a tree in the woods?' "

"No, but I was addlepated. Gramma thought I'd had too much sun."

"Really?" she asked, tilting her head upward while the sun sprinkled light and shadows on her nose like freckles. "You never told me."

"Some things you don't confess until you're confident."

"I liked you, too, but I fought it, thinking you weren't a Christian, but we discussed that. No matter how hard we fought, God let me see the Holy Spirit's gifts reflected in you and everything you did. You made my heart happy."

Her words touched him, and he drew her into his arms. "Can I kiss you now like I've wanted to for so long?"

"Please," she said. "I've waited for the same."

His lips met hers, filled with commitment and love. She returned the joy in her response, her arms closing around his neck, her fingers brushing against his hair. When they drew back, Eric caught his breath. "I think we need to keep the rest of these kisses until we're married."

"I agree," she said, a flush tinting her cheeks.

They turned back, but in few steps, Eric spotted a climbing tree, one with low limbs and wide branches. "Want to celebrate?"

"What do you mean? Aren't we celebrating?"

He motioned toward the tree. "How about a climb?"

The nostalgia touched Karen's joy-filled heart, and she ran ahead of him.

Eric watched amazed as Karen scampered into the tree and settled herself on an upper limb.

"Won't be long and I'll be too old to do this."

Or expecting our first child, he thought, but he didn't say the words. They had plenty of time to discuss important things like that.

He joined her, sitting a little closer to the Lord on the limb of an old elm tree.

"We're really out on a limb now," he said.

"Not any more. We're right where we're supposed to be." She took his hand in hers and kissed each finger. "God's awesome, you know."

"He is." Eric's memory flew back, and he turned to her. "Would you sing to me one more time?"

His question spiraled her joy to the treetops. "Do you know the song 'Awesome God'?"

He nodded. "Will you sing that for me?"

"Only if you will," she said.

"Me? I don't sing."

"You will today." She gave him a smile that warmed his heart all the way to his toes.

She began, and soon he joined in, lifting his voice into the trees. He wondered if they were close enough to the picnic area for their grandparents to hear the wonderful words that praised God for all His gifts.

When the song ended, Karen's eyebrows raised to the sky. "You have a wonderful voice, Eric. I never knew."

"No," he said. "You're just hard of hearing."

"You do, and you know it." She gave him a playful push.

As she did, Eric shifted back so she'd miss, but he realized too late. He felt his legs slipping from the limb, and he could do nothing except grab a lower branch as he slid from his perch.

"Eric," she yelled.

He grinned at her, hanging from a branch below, but his shoe had caught in the crook of a limb, and he dangled above the ground with one shoe off and one on.

When Karen saw he was fine, she laughed and started down, grabbing his shoe on the way.

Eric dropped to the ground and lifted Karen from the tree, holding his shoe.

"Isn't this where we came in?" she asked, handing him his sneaker.

"Not really." He drew her into his arms and kissed her forehead, then her nose, then brushed a kiss on her mouth. "We've come a long way since that day."

She smiled. "I guess we have."

"And we have a long way to go. . .with God's help," he said.

Karen gazed into his eyes. "A long way to go. . .together."

As they wandered back toward their grandparents, the sun's warmth washed over them like a blessing.

eighteen

Two summers later

Karen gazed into the backyard from her bedroom window, enjoying how lovely her grandfather and the Kendalls had decorated it. A large tent covered one side of the yard, filled with round tables borrowed from the church. Gramma Bea had insisted on renting white linens, and she'd arranged vases of flowers from her garden. Beneath the trees two long tables had been arranged to hold the food for the guests—hams, corn from her grandfather's garden, fresh tomatoes, an array of delicious dishes. The chairs had been arranged in neat rows in front of a trellis arch covered with fresh-cut flowers. Karen's heart thundered, knowing the day had finally arrived.

Tears filled Karen's eyes, thinking of her grandmother on this special day—her wedding. As she and Eric had known in their hearts, God had guided and blessed them. Living in Gaylord near her grandfather had added joy to her life and a sense of family she hadn't enjoyed since her parents had moved away. Eric's market had been blessed with tremendous community excitement, and Karen loved her work at My Friend's Place. Nadine had become more than her employer. She'd become her friend.

A rap on her door sent a jolt of jangled nerves through Karen's body. "Just a minute," she said, straightening the folds of her summer satin wedding gown. Her hand rose, touching the pearl-and-beaded bodice then tracing the line of the modest scoop neckline. The whole day felt like a dream as she made her way to the door, feeling like

Cinderella, except she was wearing both her shoes and they fit perfectly.

Nadine's smile greeted her. "Your dress is beautiful, Karen, and so are you. Are you nearly ready?"

"You look lovely yourself," Karen said, admiring the pastel peach gown with iridescent beads outlining the bodice. "Could you help me with my veil?"

"I'd be honored." She hurried through the door and closed it again.

Karen motioned to the hem-length veil lying on the bed, with a headpiece of netting and forget-me-nots.

Nadine carried the veil to the vanity mirror where Karen was seated. She worked carefully to attach it firmly then fluffed the netting before Karen stood. "Perfect."

"Thanks, Nadine." She looked in the mirror again and touched the headpiece, then focused on her matron of honor. "Have you talked with Eric?"

Nadine laughed. "He's pacing in the living room. He can't wait to see you."

Karen couldn't wait to see him in his tuxedo, but most of all, she longed to look into his dark, loving eyes.

Another knock made them both jump. Nadine held up one finger and inched the door open.

Karen's mother scurried inside. "You look beautiful," she said, holding Karen at arm's length then kissing her cheek. She eyed the spot her lips had touched and smiled. "No lipstick smear."

Her mother's mood made Karen smile. "How's Daddy?"

"Nervous, but excited. The pastor's about ready if you are."

Karen swallowed her emotion. Her parents had flown in from Florida and Eric's had arrived from Arizona. They were thrilled when they had finally set a date. Karen took one more look from her window at the rows of chairs. Friends from the Detroit suburbs, church family, and neighbors were selecting seats and chatting as they waited. The church's small keyboard had been placed to the side of the arched trellis, and the church organist stood nearby, ready to be seated.

"Looks like most everyone's here," Karen said, hearing a tremor in her voice. When she turned to face her mother, tears welled in her eyes. "I wish Grandma were here."

Her mother embraced her. "Me, too, but maybe the Lord's letting her look down from heaven today."

Karen wasn't sure about that, but it was a nice thought, and she loved her mother for it.

When Nadine opened the door, both women descended the stairs and shooed everyone from the house. Karen made her way slowly, so as not to trip and break a leg. After waiting so long, she didn't want to ruin her beautiful wedding.

From the porch, Karen could see Eric standing near the pastor with a long-time friend who had honored them by agreeing to be the best man. Eric's dark hair glinted mahogany highlights in the summer sun. He stood tall and lean, a bronze tan giving his face a warm glow. Perhaps it was love, instead, shining on his face.

Karen stepped onto the sidewalk as the music began, then she moved to the lawn as Nadine made her way to the front. Karen's father hurried forward, kissed her cheek, then grasped her arm and led her toward the aisle. As the bride's music filled the air, Karen and her father made their way along the white wedding runner rolled onto the grass.

When Karen looked up, Eric's eyes were focused on her. A smile curved his lips, and she felt so much love she thought she would burst. She took one small step at a time, smiling at the guests who beamed back at her.

Her heart rose to her throat when she saw Ada and the two children watching wide-eyed from a row of chairs. Karen's prayers had been answered. Ada's husband had been making progress. He'd been moved to a halfway house to receive counseling and to work, and he'd been faithfully sending financial support to the family each week. God worked miracles, and Karen prayed that Ada's life would be one of them.

Eric shifted to the center as she reached him. Her father relinquished her arm, and Eric's fingers entwined with hers. The pastor's words washed over them with a message of love, commitment, and blessing. "For better or worse, in sickness and in health, forsaking all others. . . "

Eric's hand tightened on hers, and Karen knew that God had given her a special gift. Her life would be filled forever with laughter, joy, love, and faith with the man who'd found her singing in a tree and captured her heart. In the Bible, the Lord said, "But love ye your enemies, and do good, and lend, hoping for nothing again; and your reward shall be great."

Standing hand in hand with Eric, Karen knew God had rewarded her in many ways, but especially with Eric, a husband to have and hold forever.

A Letter To Our Readers

Dear Reader:

In order that we might better contribute to your reading enjoyment, we would appreciate your taking a few minutes to respond to the following questions. We welcome your comments and read each form and letter we receive. When completed, please return to the following:

Fiction Editor
Heartsong Presents
PO Box 719
Uhrichsville, Ohio 44683

1. Did you enjoy reading *Out on a Limb* by Gail Gaymer Martin?
   ❏ Very much! I would like to see more books by this author!
   ❏ Moderately. I would have enjoyed it more if

   _____

   _____

   _____

2. Are you a member of **Heartsong Presents**? ❏ Yes ❏ No
   If no, where did you purchase this book? _____

   _____

3. How would you rate, on a scale from 1 (poor) to 5 (superior), the cover design? _____

4. On a scale from 1 (poor) to 10 (superior), please rate the following elements.

   ____ Heroine   ____ Plot
   ____ Hero   ____ Inspirational theme
   ____ Setting   ____ Secondary characters

5. These characters were special because?_____

_____

_____

6. How has this book inspired your life?_____

_____

_____

7. What settings would you like to see covered in future **Heartsong Presents** books? _____

_____

_____

8. What are some inspirational themes you would like to see treated in future books? _____

_____

_____

9. Would you be interested in reading other **Heartsong Presents** titles? ❑ Yes ❑ No

10. Please check your age range:

   ❑ Under 18   ❑ 18-24
   ❑ 25-34   ❑ 35-45
   ❑ 46-55   ❑ Over 55

Name_____

Occupation _____

Address _____

City_____ State_____ Zip_____

Presents

Great Inspirational Romance at a Great Price!

Heartsong Presents books are inspirational romances in contemporary and historical settings, designed to give you an enjoyable, spirit-lifting reading experience. You can choose wonderfully written titles from some of today's best authors like Hannah Alexander, Andrea Boeshaar, Yvonne Lehman, Tracie Peterson, and many others.

When ordering quantities less than twelve, above titles are $2.97 each.
Not all titles may be available at time of order.